WEST OF THE NULLARBOR

Stories and Verse –
West Australia 1900–90

P ETER G. C OLLINS

First published in 2004
by Serendipity
Suite 530
37 Store Street
Bloomsbury
London

British Library Cataloguing-in-Publication data
A catalogue record for this book is available from the British Library

ISBN 1-84394-074-4
Printed and bound in Europe by the Alden Group, Oxford

WEST OF THE NULLARBOR

To my family who have been its inspiration, I dedicate this volume.

Contents

Preface   ix

Foreword   xi

A Natal Day (verse)   1

The Nativity   2

The Chaffcutters   9

A Mother's Day Thought (verse)   25

Where The Boys Are   27

It's The Season (verse)   36

Mission Completed   38

Christmas Eve (verse)   62

A Breath of Country Air   63

The Judge (verse)   72

A Case of Legal Dentifrice   74

Lines Written Over One of Those Blasted Places (verse)   89

My Most Memorable Christmas   91

Nuytsia Floribunda (verse)   92

My Most Memorable Christmas (2)   93

The Spirit of Christmas   94

Christmas Dinner   95

A Christmassy Christmas Tale (verse)   99

Three Blind Mice (a skit)   101

Autumn (verse)   110

Profile of a Forebear   111

July Downunder (verse)   117

The Wages of Romance   118

A Step in Time   128

Ever After   144

Preface

I would like to preface these remarks by an assertion that the presentation of the following stories and verses is motivated rather by a desire to see myself in print than by any expectation of their acceptance. However, when I was very young, I was nevertheless sufficiently precocious to inform my English tutor that I would like to be a writer. Whether this was just a passing fancy, or a belief that such an occupation would be a means of avoiding a regular 44 hour week job I do not remember. I do recall that he gently informed me that he thought it would be very hard, which reply was quite possibly motivated by his assessment of my potential. Be all that as it may, my fascination with language was overridden by a number of factors in the ensuing period. There are many other things to interest and occupy us in the world, and the importance of acquiring the means of earning one's bread is primary, followed closely by getting the butter to put on it. Also about this time, some will remember, the world was convulsed by a contest for the supremacy of nations, and for four and a half years my attention was absorbed by that little diversion. Some years later, my uncle died; he was one of only a few relations I had got to know, since I had always lived so far away, and his grandson wrote to me saying what a colourful character he had been, and how it was a pity that he had gone, leaving no trace or record of his life for the entertainment of his descendants. That I could well understand. He could himself have told some lively tales. His grandson proposed that I should write my own story. Since then, another relative has voiced the same statement. I have not done so. I am self-conscious about writing about myself. I should feel obliged to try and steer a middle course between self aggrandisement and self denigration, and that would most probably be transparent. I haven't the outlook of the Cockney soldier who:

' ... frequent broke a barrick rule
An' stood beside an' watched me self
Behavin' like a bloomin' fool,'

nor do I have his philosophy:

'An sat in clink wivout my boots,
Admirin' 'ow the world was made.'

And I don't hope to display the Kipling skill of portrayal.

I have simply plucked a few scenes from my life, which has been longish and varied, with many changes, and made stories of them which, if nothing else, will provide a kind of narcissistic pool into which those interested can look for the sort of life I have lived, the way I have reasoned, the things that have happened to me, the things I deem important.

And it has given me an opportunity to play with words, and create pictures to convey the message.

Foreword

It is with pleasure that I accepted the invitation to write a foreword for this book *West of the Nullarbor*.

The author has been known to me for many years and he has a great respect for and appreciation of the English language – indeed, during his fifty years at the WA Bar these attributes were among his prime tools for earning his living, first as a country lawyer in the wheatbelt of Western Australia near where he grew up and later in the Port City of Fremantle. He can call upon an endless supply of experiences and long exposure to the many and varied facets of life.

Prior to these years his formative life on a farm is rich with the sights, sounds and smells of a time gone by. Of depression hardships and early struggles clearing land to grow crops and provide pasture. Of a father returned from serving in WW1 with the 10th Light Horse and of a mother newly arrived from England trying to deal with the isolation, heat, dust and hard work such as she had never imagined, cooking endlessly for farm hands, shearers and chaffcutters not to mention her own husband and five sons.

This then is the mainspring of these lovely stories, their innocence a true reflection of how things used to be, a step back to a time of quality of life, in spite of hard work. People at that time, living in an infant country, were imbued with the idea of building something for the future. However, not all of these stories and poems necessarily reflect that particular time – they bring us up almost to the present day and give us something different to think about, something to distract and amuse, an altogether refreshing look at the fabric and patterns of life. This book will appeal to the reader looking for a divertissement, time out in fact for a few moments or more from today and its vicissitudes ...enjoy.

Elizabeth O'Leary

A Natal Day

A natal day is a milestone in everyone's life,
    And jokes in poor taste about cakes and candles are rife.
So don't be surprised if I get in the queue with the rest,
    And give your susceptibilities one more test.
Tell me, why do you celebrate the end of a year
    That brings you another three hundred and sixty days near
The end of your stay on the bountiful pleasant earth? –
    It doesn't to me seem a proper occasion for mirth.
Still, if you insist and the habit you're loath to relinquish,
    I'll just lend a hand, the blaze on your cake to extinguish!

The Nativity

Jimmy Windmill lay luxuriously stretched in a prone position gazing out across the farm. That was not his real name, only some appendage frivolously attached by the white man who had entered his world, who found the unusual rolling syllables of his tribal nomenclature too cumbersome for repeated use. With them the concern was for brevity, quickness, despatch, but with Jimmy life was to live, to savour. Every fleeting moment was to enjoy and treasure forever in a boundless store of reminiscences, extracting the optimum. It was a lovely day. The easterly had sprung up cold and sharp – lazy, because it did not trouble to go round you – but the sun was rising bright and warm, sending its rays the breadth and distance of the horizon. Jimmy was having a 'day off'; he had helped the Boss load up last night – sixty three-bushel bags of premium wheat on to the great farm wagon, ready for transport to rail, and had earned his rest. It was harvest time. The farm was alive with activity. The paddocks were swaying with golden grain half stripped, and time was of the essence. The farmer didn't even want to take a day off for Christmas, which was only two days away, but the Missus said, 'Oh, but you musn't work, dear, not on Christmas Day!'

The farmer was Jack Scanion, married, with two daughters, 10 and 8. They were the apples of his eye, though he hadn't bargained for girls. He had wanted boys to help him with the farm, which he was obliged to carry on on his own. But he got some very useful assistance from aboriginal boys. He couldn't always rely on them, of course, and some rather unforeseen consequences sometimes ensued from employing them.

The horses were hitched, six of them, two abreast, standing patiently in the morning light before the homestead. The Boss had broken his fast, and was standing with the Missus at the front door. They were locked in a hurried but important discussion.

'I don't think I can,' he was saying. 'It's a day and a half into the siding, anyway, and if she gets into trouble on the way, it'll delay us on the road, overnight perhaps, miles from anywhere! Don't you think it'd be better if you handled it here?'

'Well, maybe,' was the rejoinder. 'Maybe. But I don't know everything; and with these girls, it might be all different, and I can't take the risk. Oh! Jack, she's been such a good girl, and I wouldn't want anything to happen to her!'

Sarah was an aboriginal girl and worked for the Missus. She adored her work, seeming to wish to please the Missus in every way possible. No task was too hard, none too dirty, none too tedious. She swept, scrubbed floors, polished brass, washed up, laundered, even cooked, and sewed to the best of the ability of her busy fingers if the necessity arose. She was invaluable. She seemed to have a feeling for the white man's ways, full blood though she was. The Missus was so pleased, and so proud to have her, and treated her with every consideration. She was tallish, around five feet four, slight and not so broad as the usual aboriginal girl of her build, strong, straight with long legs and arms, shapely breasts and a head well set on her shoulders. She was young, not 20 yet, so she claimed, and there was no-one to dispute the fact, since she had long since lost her parents. Her nature was gentle and sunny, she had a winning ready smile, her eyes flashed, and the long lashes swept her cheeks with the softest look imaginable. And now – she was expecting!

It was the most natural thing in the world to have happened to such a beautiful girl. The Boss was furious; he didn't blame her, he had his suspicions about this one and that one, and reckoned he had a pretty good idea who was responsible! She wouldn't spill the beans, wouldn't say a word about it or give the slightest clue. So time went on, and now the birth was imminent – so imminent that a couple of times the Missus noticed things which made her realise that something must be done pretty soon, if anything was done at all, and she asked the Boss to take her into Mrs Langdon at Moorine. Mrs Langdon was an ex-nurse who had the training and experience to deal with births. Better soon than late. The Boss did most of his business in Moorine; he bought his supplies there, paid his rates, unloaded his wheat, entrained his sheep, and generally found it unnecessary to go much further. It was a twenty-five mile journey. He only had the wagon and the spring cart, and the latter was out of commission because the steel rim had broken free of the outside wheel, and it would require the services of a wheelwright, if not a wheel altogether. He already had to bring out a list of supplies from the local co-op store backloading on the empty wagon. It was a trip which would take him two days. The first would bring him within a few miles of the siding, and if he got away early the next morning, he could get there by the time the siding opened, unload, get his stores, and in a long day's journey, with a light load, be home late Christmas Eve. Now he must try to get Sarah to Mrs Langdon – if she lasted that long.

So Sarah was invited to go in the wagon. The Missus provided a few extra items, 'in case of emergency', and the team moved off with the two on board. The Missus watched their progress as they moved along the road by the fence to the boundary of the farm, and then up the boundary road till they were obscured by thickets of trees and bush before they reached the main north road. It was a dusty track. She had done the trip many times and imagined it now again: horses endlessly plodding, puffs of dust rising from their footsteps, occasional snorts to cope with flies or dust, the wagon creaking under its load, the soft monotonous clash of the swingles, the sun bearing down, the peace and stillness of a summer's day. The horses needed water and rest and feed bags, and there was no point in pushing them to do more – 'inch by inch with the weary load'. The team made slow progress, and, looking at his pocket watch as the sun mounted overhead, the Boss stopped them at midday and unhooked the wagon chains so they could relax under a shady tree. It was a water-hole, usually conserving sufficient supplies into the early part of summer, providing winter rains were normal, to accommodate passing teams. He lit a fire to make tea. While the billy boiled he led the horses to a trough. It was cut from a tree felled and hollowed for the purpose. He'd brought a bag of chaff and a bushel of oats along with other items necessary for the trip, and he filled their nosebags. Apart from the tea, there was no need for any other preparation for lunch, as the Missus had cut sandwiches, and of these the two partook with gusto. The Boss lit his pipe.

Then it was time to be on the move again, and the afternoon wore away much as the morning. By the time the sun had fairly set, they reached their final resting place for the day. Here, the road fell into a shallow depression, and they pulled off into an open space of bare ground, surrounded by bush and not much more than sufficient to accommodate the wagon and team. On the far side, in a gully, lay a pool of clear water fed by a soak, and the Boss again unhitched the horses and led them there to drink. Then he doled out chaff and oats into nosebags and hung one over each animal's head, to the accompaniment of much appreciative snorting. He tethered them in a half circle at a safe distance from where he proposed to light a fire. Then he washed his face and hands at the soak, and set Sarah to peeling potatoes and onions while he boiled the billy. They dined simply on a tin of beef and the vegetables washed down with black tea. He laid out his own bed of hessian bags on the far side of the fire away from the horses where he could keep an eye on them. He didn't expect trouble. He usually had a bluey for himself, but decided that if the easterly sprang up again, his charge might feel chilly in the night, and so he spread it over her when she lay to rest, in between the bags of wheat on the wagon. Darkness fell quickly after the sunset, and reigned overhead and in the bush surround. It was a peaceful scene, silent save for the munching of the horses busy with their nosebags, and occasional rustlings and other noises of the bush. By the light of the fire and a hurricane lamp, the Boss threw out the remains of the billy tea, and rinsed the plates, knives and forks. By 8.30 both he and the girl were fast asleep.

He was a sound sleeper and an early riser, but it was as well on this night that he should have had his soundest sleep early, for as he lay on his back snoring, he was somewhat rudely awakened. It seemed he was being urgently patted on the chest, and he opened his eyes to look into the scared face of Sarah. She was pleading with him in a panic.

'Boss, Boss, wake um, wake um, sumpun happen me. I tink baby come. I tink baby come quick.'

His immediate impulse was to tell her to get back on the wagon where she belonged, and let him get some sleep. He was startled and alarmed himself. But he realised it was not his cue to adopt an authoritative tone. He softened immediately at the sound of her frantic voice, and seeing her terrified aspect. She was just a child. He tossed back his covering and stood up.

'Sarah,' he cried, 'get down here; you must lie down here. Put your head on my coat. Pull up your dress. Take off everything; do you hear? Make yourself as comfortable as you can. I'll make some warm water. Now, just do what you want to do.' He had no idea what she must do, and was depending on nature to take its course. 'I'll help you,' he said, helplessly enough though.

But he drew water from the spring. The embers were still alive, and with a few sticks he had a fresh blaze going, and hung the billy from the crossbar over them. Then he returned to the girl. Regular spasms were contorting her face and body now, and she gasped with the intensity of them. The baby was coming all right!

'Ho' my han', Boss! ho' my hand. He'p me.'

She was a picture of alarm and desperation as she strove to unburden herself of the load she carried. Her big eyes rolled showing vivid white against black skin. Damn shame, the Boss was thinking; she was the prettiest little lubra he had ever seen, tall and straight, flawless skin, laughing eyes, usually; she had a lovely happy outlook, and was as straight in her nature as in her body. She wouldn't lie for anything; yet forebore to disclose the identity of the father of the child she was bearing. And now this! The Boss held her hand, spoke words of encouragement, really entered into the spirit of the thing. After three quarters of an hour of struggle and stress was born the little boy as Nature intended. Both mother and the Boss breathed relief. He knew the rudiments of procedure following birth, smacking the baby's bottom, warm water, soap, dry cloths, severing the umbilical, cups of tea ... Sarah lay back on her rough billet in exhaustion and thankfulness.

'Take it easy,' he said, 'take it easy, my girl. Take the baby, and you know what to do there, and both have a good sleep. You'll be right again by morning.'

He cleared up things as best he might, and lit his pipe gratefully.

But then, as Sarah sank back with the baby nibbling at her breast, he thought, 'It's already morning!' He glanced at his watch. It was going on 3.00 a.m. He looked around him. Sarah was sleeping now, and the baby too! He took the baby from her, just in case. A spare nosebag lay on the ground. He fetched the bluey from the wagon, folded it on the feed bag, and laid the baby down. The horses, some with heads hung, stood patiently, idly surveying the little scene; all around the bush was in darkness, enhanced by the fire's soft glow; the great stars looked down; a wallaby ventured from cover to drink at the soak. The Boss lit his pipe again. He sat and watched the young mother and her son. Soon the dawn would burst from the sky in the east.

'By golly!' he said aloud to himself, as though his self was standing there in front of him, listening with full approval, 'By golly! This is Christmas.'

By 5 a.m. he was ready to be on his way. He woke Sarah, and helped, almost lifted, her on the wagon, and arranged the load so she could have a comfortable ride. They arrived at Moorine as the siding was opening. The lumper was astounded to see the passengers accompanying the load. Mrs Langdon, however, he said, had gone to Southern Cross ('the Cross') to do some Christmas shopping. 'I can't say when she might get back here,' he said, 'it might very well be some time tonight.'

The Boss had hoped and expected to be home again by the nightfall, travelling as he would be all day, with nothing aboard the wagon save his Christmas supplies, and he wanted to see his little girls before they went to sleep on Christmas Eve. He lingered a moment pondering the choice that lay before him. Sarah had given no indication of any departure from a course of swift and complete recovery. He must keep an eye on her, of course, and the baby too. He told her what he was thinking. To his eminent satisfaction, she was ecstatic about going straight home, and not a little relieved by the suggestion to overlook the visit to Mrs Langdon. It was settled, and they proceeded according to the amended plans.

The Missus was waiting dinner for them when they arrived. It was well past dusk, and it had been a long, long day. Sarah and her new arrival were welcomed and packed off to bath and bed. Jimmy was waiting for their homecoming, too. He had the broadest smile that the Boss thought he had ever seen on his cheeky black face. 'Mighty suspicious,' thought the Boss in passing; but there was so much to do, supplies to unload, horses to water, feed and stable. He could grease the wagon later. Now he had to assist with the Christmas tree, open mail, sort out presents, and have his dinner. His little girls had been put to bed, but it was a warm night, and the prospect of sleep was remote. They came bubbling out of the bedroom now, as he sat at dinner – Samantha and Tamara (Sammy and Tammy), brimming with excitement about Christmas.

'We made a nativity scene,' they chorused. 'Do you know about nativity, Daddy?'

The Boss was able to admit to a measure of acquaintance with the phenomenon. 'I'll come in when I've had my tea,' he said, 'and just see if you've got it right.'

But when he went into their bedroom in a few minutes, they were both fast asleep.

The Chaffcutters

When Caleb Short shifted uneasily on the rim of the tray of the old spring cart drawn by Banjo, the erstwhile plough horse, it was not on account of the precariousness or physical discomfort of such a position. He was inured to such things. The old cart with its metal rimmed wheels ground its way jerkily over the rough earthen track. He was on its way homewards for lunch following completion of a little job at the end of the paddock. Winter rains had flooded the creek, and the weight of water together with the debris carried along with it had flattened the netting for a chain along the boundary fence. A couple of stray sheep had drawn his attention to the damage the day before. There was always something to do. It was supposed to be a period of inactivity on the farm, but unless odd jobs were attended to at once, a stage was soon reached when things were out of control. Then the problem was where to start; and certainly there was little opportunity to deal with them when seasonal work began. It was now late August; crops seeded in June were approaching maturity, and all hands would then be required in one operation.

There was Old Dick, the teamster, who had been with Caleb for ten years, and was now in his seventies: Caleb had cleared the land and planted the first few crops on his own, gradually putting up fences and acquiring machinery and stock, until he could afford an employee. He was lucky to get Dick, an experienced teamster and a valuable man, thoroughly reliable and trustworthy, and together they had worked the farm until it became a profitable business. In that time, Caleb had a house built, and married a nurse from a country hospital; he and Mary were now the parents of two little girls. He was somewhat taken aback at the arrivals of two female children. He had taken for granted that they would be boys, who would be a help to him on the farm when they grew up: but his little girls were a treasure in any event, and a delight to come home to.

Old Dick was very comfortable with the family, all of whom, including Caleb, treated him with unusual deference. He was, however, getting old; he had led a hard life; his situation at that time was probably the most agreeable he had ever had but the vicissitudes of age were claiming him; he was nearly twice Caleb's age, and his employer at length reluctantly agreed that he must be allowed to go. It was his intention, he said, to return to his home country.

Caleb had one other farm worker; his name was Nelson; he was generally known as 'Bunny' Nelson, and he had held the job for two years. He was only 19 when he came to the farm, and quite unskilled. He had used the farm as a training ground for future occupations, and had been useful to his employer; he had himself profited in physical development. Now he, too, was contemplating leaving before Christmas. He had nothing in view, just an inner feeling that he should move back into the outer world until something else turned up in life's chequerboard of opportunities and disappointments. Employers were not hard to get, There were advertisements in the newspapers all the time: employees of the right sort were not always easy to come by.

It was mental unease, therefore, that motivated Caleb's involuntary shift on the slim hard rail of the lumbering spring cart. The prospect of being without employees to work on the farm was giving him a disagreeable sensation deep in his gorge.

He passed by the house on his way to the stables where he unharnessed Banjo and tethered him in a stall with a feed-box which he duly replenished. Then he called into the house for a sandwich and a cup of tea. The little girls were just released from correspondence lessons and their mother was putting away their books. Sybil was making up a kind of ploughman's lunch in the kitchen, and she greeted him with her usual easy smile. He liked Sybil. He liked people working for him with whom he felt easy. She was a city girl, really, but she loved the country life, and was not ever so much younger than her mistress, so that they had much in common. She had been with the family three years and a half, so the children were not much more than babies when she first knew them, and indeed her assistance to Mrs Short with the household and increased family seemed not less than essential. She was indeed lonely, in the way that young girls are apt to be when removed from the society of their peers, but it wasn't sufficient yet to make her look for change. She was plump and rosy, strong, well shaped, with a ready smile and a cheerful disposition, useful, and very much mistress of her own destiny. She had a pretty habit of blushing and dropping her eyes in apparent confusion when a man paid her a compliment. It was no more than apparent; the real confusion arose in her admirer, who automatically lost his sense of proportion, and was usually reduced to stammering out further protestations of his good opinions. Well, thought Caleb, at least there's no sign of losing her for a while. Somehow or other, the girl seemed to give him a feeling of confidence, he knew not why, that everything would turn out all right in the end, in any event.

The spring brought renewed activity to the farm as to everywhere else in the countryside. As the weather grew warmer it was more apparent that the crops had grown from strength to strength. Full-packed ears of wheat burst through the green sheaths formerly enclosing them, and before the growth had fairly begun to change colour, one paddock alongside the homestead was selected for reaping and binding. The binder, drawn by three horses, went round and round the area so neatly, leaving five or six inches of even stubble throughout, and spilling out sheaves at regular intervals for the men to stand in stooks and give the impression of a large encampment of army tents.

This was a transformation, and spelt great excitement for the children. Rabbits ran startled from the crop, and hid in the stooks or bolted for the boundary. At times, a snake, recently awakened from her winter's dormancy, was uncovered by someone scarcely less alarmed. Occasionally, a clutch of plover's or groundlark's eggs was disrupted, and the parent birds flew about peeping distractedly, while the hay-making marched on. There was more to come. The wagon was put to service with racks towering ten feet high at each end to increase its carrying capacity. Drawn by the ubiquitous horses, it moved about the field from stook to stook, while the men, with brown arms and perspiring bodies, spearing the sheaves with pitchforks, tossed them up to the stacker aloft. When filled to capacity, the load was drawn back to build haystacks. Then Mrs Short would send out billies of tea, and mugs, with scones and rock cakes for morning lunch. Sybil, under a broad brimmed straw, in flared floral skirt drawn in at the waist to show her youthful figure, carrying a billy and basket to the scene before unloading commenced, was a welcome sight to the workers. It was tiring work, pitching hay, and a break for refreshment at smoke-oh was little less than a necessity. The Boss would cut a plug of 'Dark Venus' and fill his pipe, and Old Dick the teamster filled his from a pouch replenished each morning at his bedside, and habitually carried on his person.

Hay carting was no sooner over than the chaffcutters appeared. Their job was to convert the now mature hay into chaff. Excitement, expectation, mounted as they came into view, appearing first as a kind of road train moving slowly up the boundary fence to the south and finally turning left through the gate into the access road toward the homestead. The procession was led by a steam engine drawn by two horses, and there followed a medley of vehicles, a small wagon carrying firewood, a van, a dray, the chaffcutting machine on wheels and a couple of trolleys drawn by two more horses, bearing food supplies, camping equipment, bedding and water tanks. The steam engine was black and boasted a tall smokestack, and at the head of the procession was something reminiscent of those images in the history books of James Watt's locomotive invention. The little community, four men only, was completely self-sufficing, arriving late afternoon, giving time to pitch a couple of tents, rig up a camp-fire and have a meal ere darkness had fairly settled. After dark, from the homestead could be seen by the light of the fire, silhouetted figures moving hither and thither, and it was a warm and comfortable feeling to the family to have, for once in a while, neighbours so near at hand. At night, the gang settled down to smoke, or read by the light of a hurricane lamp, and sometimes to a sing-song. One twanged a ukelele, one played a harmonica. At times they were joined in these evening entertainments by members of the homestead household.

The boss of the chaffcutters' gang, old Jim Stevens, owned the plant, lock, stock and barrel, and within the limits of a fickle labour market, had picked his employees with discrimination. He ruled them firmly and fairly. He stood marginally over six feet, but a broad chest and a slight stoop belied his stature, and he was only old, really, in comparison with the men, all of whom were under thirty. There was Cass Paterson, who played the ukelele. He was tall, spare of build, with long arms and legs, and moved with an easy grace. His face was oval and long, to match his build, with high forehead crowned by neat dark hair, usually partly hidden by a battered panama hat. Then there were Jeremy Barton, of harmonica skills, a shorter, stouter, less spectacular figure, armed with a ready flow of quiet, dry, irony, and Percy Carroll, a romantic young gentleman with a soulful expression, who nevertheless possessed a useful, practical nature and an apparently tireless capacity for work. When the gang had fairly settled down to prepare their rough evening meal, Caleb called on them to ensure they had proper access to water, and to extend the customary courtesies of the farmer towards his temporary invitees. They lived rough, and were, as has been said, self-sufficient, but it was only ordinary hospitality to make sure of that, and he would not in any event have wished to acquire a reputation otherwise. He knew Jim Stevens, too, and wanted to have a chat with him about business as well as general topics. In the brief twilight they stood thus for a few minutes, and as he moved away:

'Fancy a billy of tea about mid-morning?' he volunteered.

'Yes, sure, the boys will appreciate that,' was the reply. 'Smoke-oh about ten o'clock. 'Cos we'll be starting 7.30 sharp.'

Caleb nodded. 'We'll put it on the agenda.'

The next day dawned bright and clear, and the gang got away to a good start. From the house could be seen regular puffs of black smoke staining blue sky in accompaniment to the unusual sound of the distant muffled beat of the engine, well before the time specified by Jim Stevens. Mary Short duly went to work with pastry board and rolling pin, flour, milk and eggs, for a batch of scones to be taken hot from the oven in good time to leave the house for the men's smoke-oh. She relished the preparation of good food for appetites sharpened by activity in the fresh air, and when she handed over a neatly prepared basket and steaming billy, one could hardly be blamed for getting the impression that she felt a trace of envy of the one entrusted with their delivery to the grateful recipients.

Cass saw Sybil approaching thus laden, and sang out to Jim Stevens, who passed the last couple of sheaves on the table into the cutter and signalled back to halt the machinery. Cass threw the lever which dropped the belt from the cutter drive, allowing the engine to keep running quietly without undue loss of steam, and went forward to take the basket and billy from her hands. Their eyes met, his in delicious approval, hers in frank admiration. Old Jim did not fail to notice this first encounter, and his first impulse, quickly suppressed, was to interpose, in the interests, as he saw them, of preventing any hindrance to work. He would have been too late anyway. The die was cast. Cass invited Sybil to sit with the men while they enjoyed their ten minutes smoke-oh, and he motioned her to a seat near to which he was able to take up a position for himself. The others gathered round and most of the conversation then centred round her, faintly provocative, her presence on the farm, her marital status, relationships, hopes, a host of information indeed, all of which, thus elicited, was carefully gathered and stored by Cass. Sybil feigned embarrassment, with her little trick of dropping her eyes, but in fact was very much elated at receiving so much attention, and thoroughly enjoyed it all. The farm was not a place where she got a lot of it. She had, she began to think, almost forgotten what it was like. She had to wait, anyway, for the return of the mugs to take the things back to the house, and when the tea break ended, Cass made a point of gathering them up to hand to her, personally walking with her a few steps toward the house.

'You should come up tonight after tea,' he said. 'Perhaps we'll have a sing-song, and a bit of music,' and Sybil's eyes sparkled.

'Right, Cass, hook up the engine. We'd better get going.' The boss's voice interrupted any further exchange. But the stage was set. After dinner at the house, Sybil invariably helped to wash up and clear away. Usually, afterwards, she spent a little time in the sitting room with embroidery or crochet, but this evening she was out of the house in an instant; Mary joined her and brought her two little daughters, but could only stay temporarily, as their bedtime was looming. All were waiting expectantly at the camp, including Jim Stevens, who had elected to adopt an attitude of tolerant amusement, and they all raised a cheer as the women walked into the firelight. The ukelele player was coaxed in to service, and soon the mouth-organ also, along with a few vocal items into which Sybil joined spontaneously. It was a warm moonless evening. The shadows were velvety and impenetrable around them; for that brief hour, it was as though their whole world lay in that circle of firelight, all the rest insulated and forgotten. Sybil had never thought the country could hold such pleasures. Romance shone from her eyes, enhancing her youthful natural vivaciousness, She could not remember ever being so happy. The other two younger men were equal contenders for her attention, but when they realised that she really only had eyes for Cass, they yielded with an envying spirit and were soon on their way to retire. The boss had gone to his bunk early, warning all that they had to be up for an early start in the morning. Cass took it for granted that he should escort Sybil back to the house.

He took her arm, ostensibly so that she should not trip on some ob-struction. There were indeed, oddments of machinery, mallee roots, scattered chaffbags; it was pitch dark out of the firelight, relieved only by the stars, and the dark objects were not easily discernible, but she knew every inch of the way; he was more at risk. Nevertheless, she did not resist his guiding hand; on their arrival at the house, he drew her unresistingly close to him, and kissed her cheek; she moved her lips to engage his.

For minutes they remained thus, tightly together without a word. Then he spoke: 'Are you coming tomorrow night?' 'Yes,' she whispered, and turned and walked quickly into the house. He waited until he could see the glow of a lamp from a window. Then he strode swiftly back to the camp.

It was ages before either could get to sleep.

Cass rose early next day before the others. He was anxious not to provoke more badinage than what the boss was sure to heap on him. The boss was, however, just curious; surely the evening must have done the young fellow some good. The other two were not so restrained. Cass endured their banter with smiling fortitude. When morning tea arrived, the sly remarks erupted again. Sybil was blushing uncontrollably, but she sat out the tea break with an otherwise admirable outward control which left no doubt in anyone's mind that she was unashamedly attracted to Cass. He seemed to know this himself, and remained commendably humble as though completely satisfied with the situation.

The chaffcutters completed their job within three days. Two hay stacks had disappeared, and in their place stood a stack of bags of chaff sewn ready for the chaff shed, or sale, as Caleb should determine. It had been a busy interlude: Jim Stevens' business demanded that they should work fast and move on to the next job, and he therefore lost no time in executing his contracts. The season was short, and he must deal with as many farmers as he could, while the hay was fresh, and pack as many jobs as possible into the time available. In this way he had a quick turnover, and he paid his men accordingly. They all knew there was no time for dallying in any particular locality, no matter how brilliant the weather, or how hospitable the farmer, or how pretty the girls. The team finished punctually at sunset the third day, and after dinner and another social evening, laid themselves to rest. The firebox in the engine was cleared out, the machinery greased, oiled, and consolidated, and all save the beds and bedding, the tents and kitchen utensils, packed up ready for the move next morning. Shortly after sunrise, they were on the move again, with much less ceremony than at their arrival, or at least, that was how it seemed to the household who had their own jobs to do and had little time for interest in, or attention to, their departure.

Only Sybil looked somewhat wistful as she watched the procession trailing up the exit road. She had always involved herself in the little celebrations of the family, Christmas, birthdays, visits to this and on that occasion, and helped prepare for them with much enthusiasm, but never had she enjoyed anything so much as the little concerts in the open air, at night, sitting on a log in the company of the jocular chaffcutters. Caleb was not insensitive to her change of mood. At dinner that evening she was unusually quiet. After the soup was served, he broke into her reverie.

'You enjoyed the company of the chaffcutters, then, Sybil?' he teased.

She blushed a pretty pink; this time it was she who was confused.

'Yes,' she said, 'they were fun.'

'That young fella, Cass; he paid you a good deal of attention, I'd say?'

She flushed deeper and dropped her eyes. 'He was very nice,' she said wistfully. There was almost a tear, her eyes moist.

'We don't get many young fellas round here. I don't suppose he'll be back till next year, now, even if he's still working on the gang. They change about a bit on that job. You haven't got any ambitions in that direction, I suppose?'

'Not really.' This time her lashes were wet.

'Why, what do you mean? You haven't fallen for a chaffcutter hand, have you?' Caleb was still teasing.

She looked him straight in the eye. 'He asked me to marry him,' she confessed.

He couldn't have been more taken aback; his mouth fell open; he stared; he was lost for words, and he tried to speak but in vain. The news with its attendant possible consequences on him and the household was a blow he hadn't in the least expected. His faintly mocking air evaporated like a mist before sunshine. At length: 'He asked you – he asked you to – and did you accept?'

'No,' with contrition. He relaxed, but immediately became sympathetic. He was sensitive in these areas. The realisation of Sybil's existence, so separate, and yet so bound up with his own, came suddenly upon him. Attractive, intelligent, young, healthy, her life lay before her like a story waiting for a plot, if only a plot could be devised. He could not expect her to remain forever a servant in his house. She had her own life to live – and yet, why had she declined this offer? He was very glad she had. She had been such an asset, really part of the family, giving her assistance with compliance and initiative. He decided to take the line of least resistance.

'Oh! I'm sorry, Sybil. I didn't mean to pry. I'm just – oh, sorry,' and did not pursue the matter further. If she was going to get over it, he thought, it would be very much to his advantage, and if not, well, it was really none of his business. He glanced over at Mary, who had overheard all this exchange and could see that Sybil was upset. After dinner, she said to Sybil:

'You go in and have an early night. I'll look after the tea things.'

'Oh! It's all right,' Sybil answered lamely, but in response to further sympathetic persuasion, she did indeed repair to her room, and was later on in the evening joined there by Mary offering her consolations.

'Nothing, really, we can do about it,' Mary said to Caleb. 'We've got used to her being here, and she's become part of us, you might say. But she's young, and marriageable, and very attractive. He's eligible, certainly, in spite of being a bit light in the future stakes. She says he's just an odd-job man, and when the chaffcutting season finishes, he'll be out of a job – not a pleasant prospect; hardly a foundation for married life.'

'And that's why she knocked him back?' volunteered Caleb.

'Yes, and she's blaming herself. Thinks she made the wrong decision. They might have been able to make a go of it. She seems to be very much in love.'

'Very commendable; but practical things first. Gosh, Mary, I don't know what we'd do if we lost her, too. Dick's going home to Ireland after harvest, and Bunny wants to move on before Christmas. We'll have you out there milking the cows, you see if we don't.'

'Well, anyway, she's not going to marry him. However, I feel it's a shame. I would have wanted her to be happy; it's as if she were my own daughter.'

'Wonder where the young fella comes from,' speculated Caleb.

In the course of the next few weeks, more information was coming from Sybil concerning Cass's circumstances. He was the youngest of three brothers, with whom he had been on a family farm. The other two had married and lived with their parents, who were elderly, in a rambling old farmhouse. There was no room for another occupant. Indeed the farm had reached the limits of its capacity to sustain more people. Cass would not have been able to earn a living, and his mere presence hampered the circumstances of the others. The partnership was dissolved, and he accepted a settlement which was to be paid in cash, though he couldn't see any likelihood of being paid in the foreseeable future. He was dependent on the labour market.

Thus the picture was gradually completed, and in the course of their daily associated activities communicated to Mary by Sybil, who relished the opportunity of talking about the object of her interest. It helped her to think. Mary Short was sympathetic and helpful, notwithstanding the knowledge that she might very well be assisting the process of removing Sybil for good, something which neither she nor Caleb could wish for. She even encouraged Sybil to write to Cass, and volunteered to make enquiries for his latest whereabouts. But this was impracticable, because Sybil had signified to him that their association was at an end, and it was not her prerogative, she thought, to attempt to rekindle it. He might indeed be already otherwise happily involved. In spite of all this, in spite of herself, Mary decided to take it upon herself to try to contact him.

It was some time before this could be attempted. She planned to undertake the sole operation in secret. If she failed, she could only blame fate, and no one else would be disappointed. She had to fabricate an excuse and plan a trip to town, a rare occurrence for her, because of the distance and transport. She knew that Jim Stevens collected his mail there, and the postmaster held it for him. She offered as a reason for going to town that she wanted to choose material for new curtains for the kitchen. They certainly were overdue. She wrote a little letter.

Mr Cass Paterson,
c/o Mr Jim Stevens,

Post Office (to be called for) SOUTHERN CROSS.

Dear Mr Paterson,

If you could see your way clear to pay us a visit at Short's Farm, on the Barker Ridge Location, I think we can show you something which might be very much to your advantage.

You may remember that you were there with the chaffcutters in the middle of September.

I hope you will take advantage of this opportunity, as soon as you can.

Yours sincerely,

M Short.

She took the horse and sulky, and the little girls to give them an outing; Sybil was to go as well to help keep an eye on the children. It was a long drive and occupied a large part of the day, so it was necessary to have a lunch prepared and on the table, and dinner as fully prepared as required only heating and dishing up on their return so that a minimum of dislocation was involved insofar as it concerned the other occupants of the farm. The little pony trotted clip-clop, monotonously along the dusty bush track out on to the graded earthen road, pulling the light-framed trap with its human cargo. First stop when their destination was reached was at the water trough in the main street, then they found a shady pepper tree, where they tethered the mare and let down the shafts. The draper was not far off. Mary inspected several materials, of which there was a surprising variety: calico, drill, muslin, lace, Indian head, serge, melange, polished cotton, organdie, silk, satin, all coming off the shelves in great bolts as required. Mary knew exactly what she wanted, and was not long in choosing it. The assistant wrote out a docket, and the children were treated to the spectacle of seeing it placed in a little cup with the money their mother handed over, which was attached to an overhead wire and whizzed across the shop under the ceiling to the cashier; in a short while it came whizzing back with their mother's change and receipted bill, while they watched open-mouthed and wide eyed.

Then Mary took them all to a tiny tea shop, and ordered refreshments to be served, while she popped across the street and slipped a small envelope in the pillar box. She had played her card.

It was a day's entertainment for all four.

Spring, coaxing forth everywhere stirrings of new life, is nevertheless a fretful nurse. It is the dawn of the year, the season of youth; like many young things, it seems certain of its future one day, the next not so. Mary, hopefully awaiting a result, was even as uncertain. Her first gallant optimism was as the first warm days, when the country smiles with opening blossoms, sings with the chorus of birdsong and dances with the sudden released activity of all things: but then it was smitten by doubt as the winds and rain spitefully proclaim the last gasps of a dying winter; spring, indeed, is all things from doubt and petulance to maturity and contentment, progressing from day to day as the soft cadences of temperature slowly give way to confident summer warmth. During the whole of this metamorphosis, Mary's letter lay in the post office, gradually smothered by incoming postal items, letters with windows, letters with cheques, personal letters, notices, all awaiting the attendance of the addressee, who during any of this time might have been anything up to two hundred miles away, and with him, his gang. When the work was finished, he was at liberty to attend to business; the men were paid off, equipment stored, and all would then be looking for further occupation and lodgement.

That was how Cass Paterson found himself when he received Mary's letter.

His movements had been continuous since the job at Short's; he had been to a number of locations and the experiences, pleasant or otherwise, he had had there, seemed away back in the past. He hadn't derived anything from them save a feeling of slightly dampened spirits, injured pride, and a disappointment he strove to conceal from himself. He still doubted whether he should have accepted Sybil's refusal. He had not had a chance to make another sally. It was now nearly three months ago. He knew she had been interested. He could not believe her refusal was final. However all that might be, the letter made no allusion to that aspect. It was, as he saw it, clearly a job offer. There weren't many jobs he couldn't do on a farm. He surely couldn't lose by paying a visit. It was twenty miles from town. He would try to hitch a lift from a wheat carter.

It was nearly mid December, and harvesting was well under way at Short's. They were short-handed because Sunny had departed. Caleb had forewarning that this would be the case, but he had not had time to look for a replacement, and was hoping he and Dick could handle it. Dick was on the harvester in the south-west paddock, and as he moved the team up westerly towards that corner, he could not help noticing the lone figure approaching. It climbed through the fence, and crossed the tall stubble. Then it signalled to him, and he reined in the team.

Cass had seen Caleb Short once, but they had never met and he couldn't remember him. He assumed it was he who was driving the harvester.

'Are you Mr Short?' he shouted.

'No. You looking for him?'

'Yes. Can you tell me where I can find him?'

Dick's sweeping glance took in the tall gangling figure, neatly clad in dungarees and rough drill work shirt, and guessed the visitor's mission; he would have been well pleased to see an additional hand on the farm.

'He's round at the dump on the far corner. Jump on and I'll give you a lift.'

'Thanks.' Cass climbed across the drawbar of the machine and ensconced himself on the steering mount, and with a couple of words to the horses, Dick moved them on. There was no opportunity for further conversation. When they reached the dump at the opposite corner of the stubble, they stopped, and Cass jumped off and addressed Caleb.

'Mr Short?'

'Yes?'

'I'm Cass Paterson. I believe you're looking for a man.'

'Yes, I want a man to help me with the bag sewing and wheat carting right now. In a couple of weeks I'll be wanting a teamster.' Caleb was studying Cass as he spoke. 'Weren't you here with the chaffcutters a while ago?'

'Yes, I was here with Jim Stevens.'

'What do you know about farming?'

'Been on a farm all my life.'

'Have you? How old are you, then?'

'Twenty-eight.'

'Oh, well, you ought to have some experience. Where were you on a farm?'

'Boodarockin.'

'Oh, yes. I think I heard something about that. How d'you know I wanted a man? I've only just lost the last young bloke.'

Cass looked Caleb up and down questioningly. 'I got the letter,' he said, at length.

'Letter! What letter? Did I write you a letter? I must be getting absentminded. Have you got the letter on you?'

Cass fished it out of a breast pocket and handed it to him. Caleb read it eagerly, recognising the writing at once. 'Mary!' he breathed. He looked at Cass. 'Have you had lunch?' he queried.

'No. But look, if you didn't know about the letter, perhaps I'd better not hang around. I don't want to cause any trouble.' Cass was beginning to fear that his presence there was unwarranted after all.

He knew nothing of the relationship between this man and the writer. He wished he'd left the letter behind.

'Trouble! my boy. Trouble!' Caleb could be hearty on occasions. 'No question of trouble, I assure you. This could be the best thing that's happened this year.' He put his right hand on the other's left shoulder. 'You come and have a bit of lunch and we'll talk it over. Dick won't knock off just now. The wheat is stripping well and he wants to get as much behind him as he can. He's retiring. That's when I'll have no-one to give me a hand. Have you driven a harvester?'

'Yes, plenty. Only the "Sunshine", though. I haven't been on the AL.' The Sunshine harvester was fairly standard equipment on the wheat belt farms. The comb gathered in the heads to the beaters which swept them back to the winnower. The grain sifted through to the tray and was taken up by elevator to the bin, and the husks were blown out behind. The wheat stalks lost their brittleness in cool or humid weather, and the comb could leave them behind, but the AL (header) was fitted with knives under the comb which ensured maximum stripping. It had just come on the market. This man knew a thing a thing or two, obviously.

'You might be just the very man we need,' said Caleb. 'Come into the house and have a bit of lunch.'

They entered the house by way of the kitchen, a rectangular room with a long jarrah table, where Caleb was wont to have his meals with others of the family and the men. Sybil had not expected him so early, and was puzzled slightly by the sound of voices indicating more than one arrival. She saw Caleb come through the door, holding it open for another to follow; and at once he spoke.

'Sybil, I've got a visitor for lunch. Is Mary about?'

She gazed at them both for a moment in stupefaction, and the colour left her face; remembering herself, 'Yes,' she said, 'she's out in the garden with the children. Shall I get her for you?'

'Oh, I'll go. Perhaps you could make us some tea. Oh, and I beg your pardon; this is Mr Paterson. I believe you may have met. Cass, will you take a seat? You're probably ready for a cup of something after that trip this morning. I'll just go and get my wife.'

And he left them.

Just like that.

He went through the house to the rear, where Mary had picked a few tomatoes and was now standing with the children by the fig tree in the north-east corner. He walked over and Mary expressed surprise at the sight of him.

'Caleb, aren't you a bit earlier than usual? I don't think Sybil will be quite ready with lunch.'

'That's all right. I've seen Sybil. Mary, we've got a visitor. I'd like you to come up.'

'A visitor! I can't receive visitors.' She looked in dismay at her garden soiled hands, and apron. The little girls were looking at their father excitedly. They were similarly grubby.

'Don't worry; he probably won't notice it. Wash up a bit if you want to, but come up anyway, right away.'

'Who is it?'

'Some chap you wrote to about a job, you remember?' Caleb affected ignorance of the matter.

'Wrote to, about a job?' Mary knew she hadn't applied for work. But then the reality entered her mind.

'What's his name?'

'Cass Paterson, one of the chaffcutter blokes.'

'Cass Paterson! that was three months ago. Caleb, I wrote to him for Sybil, 'cos it wasn't up to her to do it. Does he want a job?'

'Sure, that's what he came for, not to see Sybil.'

'Where is he now?'

'Up in the kitchen. She's making him a cup of tea.'

'Phew! You did that on purpose, didn't you? Are you going to give him a job?'

'Mary, he's got all the qualifications. I need someone badly, and I'd be a fool not to take him on; and Mary, you brought him here, and I'll just drop the responsibility fair and square in your lap!' and he burst into a gale of laughter which he had been holding back too long.

'Oh, Caleb!' Mary wilted; and there, by the old fig tree, in the middle of harvest on that clear hot summer's day, they put their arms round each other.

Then each took the hand of one of the children, and they walked up to the house together.

Cass and Sybil both had the feeling of being thrown in at the deep end together, and for some time, save for the merest courtesies, scarcely spoke. Eventually:

'I got a letter,' he said.

'Oh?' she said.

'I thought it was from Mr Short, but it seems it was from his wife. It is a job offer.'

'Really!'

'Yes, but he agrees with it. He seems to be in a a bit of a spot at the moment.'

'Are you going to take the job?'

'Well, I'm looking for a job. It's nice to be offered one, and I'll be glad to take it.'

She made no reply.

'I hope you don't mind.'

'I think it would be wonderful.' She looked directly at him as she said this, and he knew his wanderings were over.

'Old Dick's been with me ten years,' Caleb was heard to say that evening. 'He's been a good man and hard to replace. If you can be anything like him, there's a future here. That adjoining property the bank foreclosed on, can be cleared of the mortgage and taken over, You and I can farm the two together. How does that suit?'

It suited fine. Sybil already had ideas along those lines.

A Mother's Day Thought

As time goes by, it seems to me
    I'm learning more and more
About the meaning of the world
    And what we're living for.

I notice hosts of little things
    As though they all were new;
The countless pieces of advice
    You hoped I'd listen to.

I hear upon the winds of time
    Your anxious voice and low
And yet above all else around –
    'Mind now, dear, how you go.'

I never take a bath, or cross
    A busy street, you know
But what I hear your voice a-calling
    'Mind dear, how you go.'

When I was young, I thought the world
    For me alone was fashioned;
I never ever thought that health
    And strength and time were rationed.

I had a mind to squander all
    That God to me had given,
And that I shouldn't was the goal
    Towards which you have striven.

It's a comfortable feeling
    Just having you to care,
And knowing you'll watch out for me
    At all times, everywhere.

And now I'm old, my life, my work,
    The few things that I've got,
It's you, my angel guardian
    To whom I owe the lot.

And still, whene'er I have to make
    Decision, yes or no,
It's never made, but first I hear
    'Mind now, dear, how you go.'

Where The Boys Are

Keeping cool in the bush on a summer's day is an art; if you can do so, it is probably because you don't get anything else done; it's a full time occupation. Keeping food cool is a necessity, otherwise it is unpalatable, if it doesn't soon putrefy. Over the years, several methods have been employed to keep food cool. The hotelier at Grass Patch used to lower a quantity of beer in a sack down a well on the property, and draw it up every time a traveller called for a drink. The most common means used by the householder was the Coolgardie safe, a galvanised iron contraption with sacking sides. The metal safe was extended upwards to form a tank to hold water, and when strips of flannel were immersed and hung over the sides, the water seeped up and ran down the hessian. Evaporation provided a cool interior on the hottest day for butter, cheese, milk, vegetables, meat and desserts.

With the march of progress, when ice began to be available from local stores, the old methods were supplanted by the ice chest. This could be kept in the kitchen, as it didn't need the assistance of natural breezes; but a block of ice could not be expected to last more than a week, so regular replenishment was necessary. The first refrigerator was a huge, ungainly wooden box fitted with a removable, cast iron double cylinder, one part of which could be heated each day with a pressure lamp. An hour's heating of one cylinder generated freezing in the other, which could then be replaced in the box, and this was very effective. It did not enjoy sustained popularity because it was cumbersome, and soon gave way to the kerosene refrigerator. This was similar to the modern article in appearance, but it had some drawbacks, such as smeeching, smelling, and requiring regular replenishments of fuel.

Households with private power supply were ready to take the electric refrigerator, when it first appeared, but it was not until the grid electricity supply was generally available that the refrigerator became common in the country.

On the farm, the first of the species arrived at Christmas, 1946.

The boys were all home from the war, except Dick, who had been too young to go, and Tim, who had walked off the ship sent to bring troops back from England, on the excuse that it was too crowded, though the truth was that he was not yet ready to leave his girlfriend.

The refrigerator arrived by rail. The Old Man got notice of its arrival, and gave his orders accordingly. Dan and Dick, he decreed, could catch and kill a couple of chickens. The free range cockerels had met with this fate each Christmas, from as far back as any of the boys could remember, and Dan was 26. They were to be plucked and drawn, the Old Man said. He knew the artfulness of the characters he was dealing with, and laid it on the line in the manner of one who was accustomed to having his orders obeyed, his word respected. Ric and Ed, 21 and 20 respectively, were to shift the last of the wheat in the dam paddock, it being already bagged and sewn, and cart it to the siding. There were thirty bags, and it would take all the morning at least, and then they were to run into town and take delivery of the refrigerator. It was a drive of twenty-five miles, and they could take the truck, an old Ford T. They set out soon after lunch.

Dan was not exactly rapt about having to stay at home on Christmas Eve. He had much rather be off with the boys, or somewhere else where he could mix with the locals of his own age, and entertain them and boost his own ego at the same time with a continual stream of badinage and idle jest. But over his years he had developed some small sense of family responsibility, and accordingly remained to carry out his father's wishes, aware that he would enjoy Christmas dinner as well as anyone else, and anyway he hadn't been invited out; so he contented himself with delivering a barrage of more or less deprecating abuse to Dick about the farm, and the job, and the Old Man, and everything else that occurred to him which didn't fit in with his current wishes. Even Mother came in for a modicum of mild vituperation when she emerged from the kitchen to urge haste in preparing the chickens, as they were required to undergo further processing after the plucking was completed, such as washing, singeing, stuffing and stitching, ready for the oven in the morning. She was aware that Dan and Dick were not overly expeditious in getting on with jobs.

This was Dan's fault. He was capable of doing any job very well, if he tried, but when he was engaged for a task on which he hadn't a current interest, he performed it dilatorily or badly, and got in the way of anyone who tried to help him. His father, the Old Man (Old Joe, as he was known in the district to his contemporaries), was past middle sixties, and had all his life been, and was still, a hard worker, thorough: a perfectionist, you could say, but it was a pattern into which Dan did not exactly fit. It grieved the Old Man sorely to have a son so incorrigibly remiss at everything except popular music, socialising, and generally acting the goat. He thought he was a bad influence on the younger sons anyway. If he broke them up and sent off Ric and Ed in the truck, at least there was a degree of segregation, and he himself could stop at home and keep an eye on things. For his own part he had just finished harvesting round the dam, and was in the process of shifting the machinery to the bottom paddock. This was half a day's work by the time he had oiled the harvester and refuelled the old Case tractor. He hadn't intended to work in the afternoon. There had been late rains in the season, and a humid change had set in, and the crop ears were unusually tough; he had ordered a header but supplies were delayed indefinitely after the war; the harvester would have left wheat behind on the stalks; anyway it was Christmas Eve.

Meanwhile the boys were proceeding to town in high spirits; they were still hot from the morning's wheat carting, and invigorated by the exercise. They arrived in the little town just after 3 p.m. It was a warm humid day. The summer sun was beginning to have some sting in it. There were cars and utilities, with the occasional truck parked along the footpath kerbing and on the other side, under the shade of trees by the station yard, several horse-drawn vehicles. A considerable number of people were shopping, mostly ladies, whilst men stood about and chatted, or carried supplies from the shops. Children were on holiday from school, and there was an air of gaiety, excitement and anticipation in the street. It was colourful, lively, bustling and joyous. Ric and Ed sensed the magic straight away. Ric, automatically it seemed, pulled the truck to a stop right outside the hotel.

'I think we might get into the spirit to start with. What do you reckon?'

he challenged, and Ed didn't demur. On the way in they ran into Ned. He was just coming out. Ned lived on the south side of the rail, opposite to Ric and Ed, who were to the north. They had been at school together.

Ned said, 'I was just looking for some of the crowd. Don't know anyone in there. Ya gonna have one?'

Ric said, 'Sure, we just been carting wheat. We're pretty dry.'

'Oh! Good. Come on then. W'at cha doing in town?'

'Come in to pick up a fridge. Over at the station.'

'Oh, right. Ya got the truck? We'll just knock one over, and I'll give ya hand on with it.'

'Good man!'

While they were thus 'knocking one over' Dave showed up at the entrance to the bar. Ed said, ''Strewth, here's Dave. This could get interesting. Come on over and have one, Dave. We just got in.'

They all welcomed Dave, who was from a farm near the Old Man's. The time passed very pleasantly; they were all hungry and thirsty, conversation warmed up, and no-one was in a hurry to leave. While they were enjoying their third schooner, each buying in his turn for the rest, they were joined by Nic and his man Terry. They came from a smallholding on the main road which Ric and Ed had passed on the way in. They were all basking in the security maintained by those who had stayed behind in the past six years, while they themselves, or most of them, had been away to protect it. One or two more and Dave said they must have one for the road, and so the end of the session remained a little bit up in the air.

Back at the farm, Dan had caught the two cockerels and tied their legs. This had involved a great deal of flurry and a circus of frantic, fleeing, farmyard fowls, much squawking and feathers flying, and pursuers and pursued ended being hot, dusty and breathless, but with Dick's assistance, the two roosters designated by Mother were, one by one, cornered and secured. Dan got the axe and carried one over to a log at the woodheap.

'Hold his head, and stretch his neck over the log,' he said to Dick.

Dick looked at him rather doubtfully at this. However, he put out his hand and took a grip of the beak, pulling the head towards him, the body lying on the other side of the log.

Dan raised the axe and was in the act of aiming a mighty blow at the neck of the bird. As the axe began to move, Dick seized suddenly by the instinct of self-preservation, let go the beak. The rooster pulled away and tucked it towards its breast. Frustrated, Dan halted the blow in mid-air.

'Hold the flamin' thing!' he expostulated.

Dick giggled nervously, but he took the head again, while Dan aimed another blow. The same thing happened. Four attempts were made to get it right. Finally the rooster's head came off clean, and then the body went hopping and fluttering around the yard aimlessly, in spite of the trussed legs, releasing its final nervous energy, and spraying the area and anyone who got in its way with its blood. Finally, Dan collared it, and hung it feet first on the clothesline to bleed.

Then followed a similar performance with the second bird.

After the two fowls were reasonably drained, but before they had grown cold, they were taken down to be plucked. This was done in the wash-house. It was a long, tedious business, not at all suited to Dan's temperament, and he kept up a steady stream of semi–insulting remarks to Dick, to relieve his exasperation, until Dick gave him back some 'cheek' of his own. Dan responded to this with threats of violence, and that ended by him chasing Dick round the yard to execute them; and Mother, who came in while they were thus absent, seeing the birds lying there, both half plucked, with the blowflies singing over them and the floor covered with feathers, vowed she'd jolly well do them herself, and she stripped the wings, which were the hardest part, took them into the kitchen, and proceeded to draw them, singe off the down, wash them and stuff them with the mixture she had been preparing.

Dan, glad to be so far relieved of this responsibility, rounded up Dolly, the pony, saddled her up and rode off in the direction of the settlement where he could meet his mates, leaving the wash-house floor to be cleaned up by Dick.

Dick was left alone with Mother, but that was all right, because they always got on very well together, and he could help her in the house too. As the afternoon wore on, the Old Man came in and had a cup of tea, his mind still on the unfinished harvest and other farm problems, and so not yet sufficiently relaxed to contemplate Christmas Eve and Day.

'Those boys should be back by now,' he reflected, 'they've been away long enough to get into town and back.'

Mother agreed. She had set Dick to peeling oranges. She wanted to have a big dish of sliced oranges and some jelly and cream for Christmas dinner, and these delectables could not be adequately presented unless they were properly chilled. So she could do with that refrigerator, even though she had done without one on prior occasions, and done very well besides. It was all very well, she reasoned, to go for the traditional Christmas feast (roast fowl – already on the assembly line, a cushion of bacon, gravy, potatoes, pumpkin and greens – all on the way) but when it came to dessert, though she had made a plum pudding (plum duff, the Old Man called it) and brandy custard, was it not nice to have an acceptable alternative? For who in this climate, could face pudding, after a generous helping or two of chicken and ham and the trimmings. It was clear that a cold dessert might be more welcome, and she had never been wrong about that. The pudding got eaten anyway, at a later date. Five boys would see to that! There was mead, too, made with honey, raisins and grain, fermenting in the old bread crock. Well, she supposed something had held the boys up.

'Hmmm,' said the Old Man, and his tone was laced with cynicism.

The trouble seemed to emanate from the simple fact of getting involved in a game of darts, There were Ric and Ed, and Dave and Ned, and Nic and Terry, and they formed teams, appointing captains and electing sides. There was a great deal of tossing coins to decide priorities, and much bonhomie. There was regular sipping, a great deal of argument about whose turn it was to buy, because this was continually being forgotten in the progress of the game, and by closing time at 9 p.m. everyone had had enough, and no one had had lunch. Ric suddenly remembered the purpose of his trip. 'We'd better go and pick up that fridge!' he said.

'Cripes, yes,' said Ed, 'nearly forgot all about it. Say, Ned, are ya gonna give us a lift on with it?'

'Sure, I'll come over,' and the three got in the old truck. After some cranking, the motor obediently started. It was not always so compliant, and one might have suspected that it was anxious to get home after such a long wait.

Many shops had closed, and the crowds had disappeared. Some had gone to the cinema, some to parties, but most had gone home, and the street was deserted.

Nic said, 'Hey, Ric, can you give Terry a lift home? I have to go round and pick up some stores.'

'Oh, yes, and I'd like a lift too,' said Ned. 'Dad's taken the car.'

'Yeah. Get on board. The more the merrier,' was the reply. 'You coming with us, Dave?' And having seen them mount the tray, Ric drove off to the railway station. The refrigerator was in a rough timbered case standing conspicuously in the dim light on the platform, where it had been unloaded from the guard's van on the passenger train a couple of evenings previously. It was a heavy, cumbersome item, but with five men to handle it, no great problem presented itself, despite the consumption by all of a considerable quantity of tanglefoot. The brothers sat in the cab with Ric as driver, and the three passengers on the tray on the way home. They were in good spirits, and an attempt was made at a sing-song, though this could not be sustained. They had to pass through three sidings on the way. The first was in complete darkness. At the second, Ric yelled out, 'We are now approaching the hotel!' thereby provoking a healthy raucous shout of 'Hooray!' As the old truck chugged by, Ric shouted again, 'We are now passing the hotel,' and the response was now somewhat weaker, more inebrious, and definitely less enthusiastic. 'Boo,' someone said faintly. They moved out of the dim light of that village into the dark of the night beyond, and the passengers relapsed into somnolence.

The next village was in utter darkness on their approach. Ned, Dave and Terry had dropped off completely to sleep on the tray, despite the discomfort of such a ride. Ed, in the absence of any necessity to keep awake, was nodding in the passenger's seat, and Ric, by the time they had reached the pier to cross the salt lake on the way to the siding, was dropping off himself, hands still on the wheel, chin resting on his chest. The front wheels deviated somewhat from the preferred track followed by previous transport, and led the vehicle across the shoulder of the road, putting it on a noticeable incline to the left, and suddenly all this was interrupted by a shout from the tray.

'Look out the fridge!'

The warning came from Ned, who had waked in time to see the big wooden box slide gently across the tray. Despite his apparently comatose state, he sprang up, but was too late to prevent it reaching the raised edge, from which it tipped and toppled gently but inevitably over into the shallow salt water and mud of the lake.

Ric was jerked into consciousness in time to prevent any further progress down the slope and pulled the wheel to guide the truck to a safer position on the pier. Ed nearly fell out of the open cab. Ric cut the motor, and they got out to survey the result. The five stood looking at the great wooden case lying on its side in a few inches of muddy salt water, for the moment speechless. They had far too recently been at great pains to load it from the firm platform of the rail station, now to be obliged to reload it from the muddy, slimy lake. The pier was only three feet high, and the water but a few inches deep. But the mud was terrible. There emerged shortly a medley of suggestions about retrieving the goods. It was a gloomy prospect. It was late Christmas Eve and the refrigerator was needed at home, from which they were still eight miles distant. It was a good six feet lower than it had been a few minutes before. Footwear had to be removed and trousers rolled before venturing into the water. Paddling in the salt lakes ensures that the feet sink four or five inches into thick clay mud, which squelches up between the toes, more with the weight of a load, and progress is slow. Five pairs of hands manhandled the package from the floor of the lake up the slope to the road surface of the pier. A good helping of mud was spread at random across feet, knees, arms and clothes. Finally, with an almighty heave, it was restored to its former place on the tray, this time lying on its side.

The passengers were unloaded at various points on the remainder of the route, two at the village and one at a farmhouse. Then Ric and Ed proceeded home. They didn't go to sleep again.

The dogs knew the sound of the old truck and were silent. The Old Man's snores reverberating through the homestead were the first intimation to the boys that the family was in bed and fast asleep, though Mother and Dan both averred the next day that they had heard them come in.

The Old Man was first up in the morning. He lit the fire in the range, made tea and took a cup in to Mother. From the kitchen window he could see the refrigerator in its box lying on the back of the Ford.

'The fridge has come, Mother,' he called out.

'Oh! I'm so glad, Joe. Now we can have some nice dessert. Are the boys all right?'

The boys were awakened by the sound of the Old Man stomping round the house. He wasn't big, but he certainly made his presence felt. They rose and went out to give him a hand with unpacking and installing the refrigerator. The Old Man couldn't believe his eyes when he got a closer look at its case.

'Great Scott!' He had used the expression since his youth. 'Great Scott! Look at all that blasted dirt. It must have been lying out in the mud somewhere.'

It was a pertinent observation, but the boys weren't drawn by the suggestion.

It's The Season

Shortly that season will commence
When peace and goodwill start to make some sense.
Folks will be nice to one another –
You'll hear them say 'pal' and 'mate' and 'brother'.
Tradesmen get very friendly with you,
Pretend to forget your account's overdue,
And even the chap that overcharges
Astounds you with unaccustomed largesse.
Fellas will slap each other's back –
'How're you, Bill?' 'I'm fine, thanks, Jack!'
And when it's for drinks your competitor rings,
Don't wonder if you're just hearing things.
It's all in the shade of the Christmas Tree
That you get these expressions of bonhomie.
Everyone comes down from the shelf –
Tomorrow, well, it can take care of itself.
Dust down the cobwebs from the bottles,
Fill up the fuel tanks and open the throttles!
So I figured since there's so much to do
I'd be off to an early start with you.
For reasons we needn't go into now
For those that can't, let's show them how.
Oh! That's very nice, don't mind if I do, thanks,
Just fill it up to the same as you, thanks.
Oh! and if you don't know, and you haven't guessed it,
No water with mine, I just detest it.
Mm, mmm, well, that didn't touch the sides.
Now another to show your bona fides.

No, that's not too much, I can manage it.
Well, things seem to be improving a bit.
Since Christmas is coming along apace
Here's one for the jolly old human race.

Mission Completed

She lay inert, quiescent as in sleep. Her life, dedicated, hard, self-immolating, purposeful, was at an end. The spirit was ready to depart.

She had that for which to be thankful; was there room for regret? In the haphazard journey through material existence, the exigencies of life, the contingencies, the stringencies of need, could one always be relied on to do the right thing, always to take the most advisable course, always to resist the inevitable, always to foresee those pitfalls the avoidance of which would materially alter the course of one's progress?

Seldom had she been blessed with material support, but she had ambition she struggled to achieve. You might from time to time have heard her quiet voice reiterate:

It isn't the things we do,
It's the things we leave undone
That give us a bit of heartache,
At the setting of the sun.

She had cause for some complacency. Her son, the object of her striving, had taken his place in the world, and was independent. She was justly proud of him.

Her work was done; her life had not been in vain.

Now in the very dusk of her decline, she had a single pang. There was one thing missing from his life – the single all-important quality of happiness.

For without happiness, there is no purpose.

Now the spirit was to have free play to roam in that ethereal sea of composite multiple force, of indestructible energy, which is the mainspring of the universe.

The little spirit departed and embarked on a mission.

* * *

Jasper had a rule which served him in much good stead, which was that on leaving his office, he promptly put out of his mind everything, except that he was obliged sometime to return, in connection with it. It was on this account, when he stepped out, as he said to Marilyn, for a spot of lunch, and she told him that Miss O. was coming in at one, that he promptly forgot all about it. Marilyn, a competent, attractive brunette of 18, was his secretary, and customarily went to lunch at one. So that the office should not remain unattended in the middle of the day, he took his lunch break half an hour or so earlier.

It was the middle of January, a warm but by no means unbearable day. Fremantle streets were thronging with business folk, shoppers and visitors. The Australian pound, not yet decimalised and demoralised to two dollars, was still a unit of currency of some significance. People talked of thousands of them with the same sense of mystery as today they speak of millions. Jasper French was a lawyer. He was an orphan, in as much as that description can be applied to a gentleman well past the first flush of his youth. His mother who, during his lifetime, had devoted her resources to ensuring her son's future, had been the last to make her exit, having met her demise a couple of years previously. He had been devastated by her loss; he had always felt secure in the knowledge of her presence; he had always shared with her his problems, large and small, and derived comfort and guidance. He still felt her influence in all he did, in all that happened to him, as though she were, in some mysterious way, still present in person, in the air around him. He had made acquaintance with the coastal city some five years now, in the course of a somewhat longer involvement in the legal profession. The appearance of his practice did not reflect its worth. His files and accounts were unwieldy and cumbersome, but nothing was ever lost or unaccounted for in his office. His rooms were shabby and untidy, with a paucity of furnishings, but his clientele, large or small, were not discouraged. He preserved an aloofness from up-to-date business systems and modern accounting equipment amounting almost to a paranoia, largely on the ground of expense. His stubborn resistance to overheads was a source of amusement to his colleagues and amazement to his business associates. Now it spilled over into his midday break. He usually did not take lunch unless a client insisted on buying it. He quite properly thought, after a nourishing breakfast and looking forward to a substantial dinner, that he did not need lunch. It was sufficiently agreeable to him to stroll the streets, indulge in the merest snack, and give himself the impression, at least, of separating morning from afternoon. It was habitual, it seemed essential. Today the warmth of the summer weather demanded nothing more elaborate than an ice-cream. Armed with this, the same discreetly camouflaged in a paper bag, having thoroughly disabused his mind of the morning's problems, he made his way casually back to his rooms, climbed the stairs, and on entry was intercepted by Marilyn.

'Miss O. called while you were out,' she said, in confidential tones. 'She came in just after you left, so I took the liberty of showing her into your office.' She looked at Jasper for approval. 'I thought she would be more comfortable there,' she added, by way of explanation.

Jasper heard this information as one hearing of a volcanic eruption in Hawaii, or a snowstorm in Siberia. It all seemed to come from far away, as though not affecting him. His mind, at that moment entirely absorbed by thoughts of strolling in warm Fremantle streets, with the contemplated pleasure of planting himself in his swivel chair and giving himself over to the enjoyment of a tasty treat, was not immediately receptive to this gentle, though forcible, reminder of responsibility. It was unusual for Marilyn to adopt this procedure. She customarily asked clients to take their seats in the waiting area. She had a business head, and it came to him that she had used it to deter the client from going elsewhere. People were unpredictable. She was aware that Jasper was not always as punctual as he might be. He was somewhat at a disadvantage now. She glanced at the paper bag. It was a small white bag and the warmth of the day was already persuading it to exhibit signs of its contents. His nod to Marilyn's words and manner signified an appreciation which he had not yet had time to develop. He went into his office automatically, as the pendulum swings back.

What he saw on entry momentarily arrested his progress. Sitting in the chair opposite his, immediately confronting him, was a girl, not more than 22, of engaging appearance, steadfast, with plump cheeks and laughing eyes. Though seated, he could see that she was tall, not willowy but of more than usual grace, attributable in large part to simple dignity. She, like him, wore a hat, and was well, though not expensively, dressed. All these things had a salutary effect on Jasper. When he made his entry thus, she looked at him with an expression which showed that she took in the situation in its entirety. The ice-cream, reposing in its little bag, so recently an object of pleasant contemplation, suddenly deteriorated into a lugubrious superfluity.

'Good afternoon,' he said.

It was as much an attempt to divert her attention from this encumbrance, as a move to initiate contact. She responded with encouraging pleasantness, though her mouth, in framing her reply, was not entirely successful in disguising a certain good-humoured amusement.

'It's quite warm outside,' he went on, taking off his hat; for this he had to find a suitable repository; his client was barring its customary route to repose. He gingerly laid down the paper bag. He found himself wondering why he hadn't eaten the ice-cream in the outer office before entry. He certainly felt funny about eating it there and then. Before the average client, he would have made no bones about it; he would have disposed of it in the course of desultory conversation, and then proceeded with his business. Somehow, now, it seemed scarcely business-like in the presence of this – this – apparition. If the interview was not long, there was a chance that it might be over ere it had disintegrated entirely and spread itself across his desk in a milky blot. But Miss O. was of a more practical turn of mind.

'Eat your lunch,' she said, 'I don't mind. I think you should.'

He could not but be grateful for this encouragement. Unprofessional or not, he took up the bag again, removed the contents, and disposed of them as efficiently and as quickly as might afford the minimum of inconvenience to his client, though not oblivious of the turn of events which had resulted in him taking advice from her, whereas she was there, presumably, to obtain advice from him. Neither was he unconscious, as he ate, of her steady gaze, and she was constrained to avert it to the window to disembarrass him. But his ordeal was soon ended, and he turned to the raison d'être, his client's business.

I'm sorry for that delay,' he said. 'Now what might be the purpose of your visit?'

Miss O. was a British migrant. She had been in Australia three months. Employment, if it meant dependence on the whim of business proprietors, or the impersonal relationship of Government departments, was not to her taste, and she was desirous of setting up her own enterprise. She had conceived the notion of establishing a Devonshire teas outlet in North Fremantle, and she wanted to know what municipal or other governmental controls might affect her operations. It was a simple administrative matter, disposed of in a few minutes with discussions of business methods, bank requirements, accounting and taxation. The interview was at an end, but Miss O. showed no sign of making her departure. The conversation continued along lines of mutual interest, as each found in the other a common ground. Jasper quizzed her about England, with which he had some connection. He had been born in London, but his mother, whose presence, incidentally, in their immediate surrounds he currently felt, had brought him to West Australia while he was still a small child, and he had since paid a visit there in service with Australian Expeditionary Forces. As it is human nature always to wish to be somewhere else, he cherished furtive ambitions one day to retire there, and never having availed himself of Australian citizenship, though his residence qualified him to do so, still considered himself English. The majority of citizens of the United Kingdom journey but little from their immediate surrounds. Apart from her foray into Australia, Miss O. was no exception to this home truth, and he felt some small advantage over her because he had been almost the length and breadth of the British Isles by plane, ship, train and omnibus. But she spoke with feeling about her home in Devonshire, where he hadn't been at all, and made him feel in some strange way, that, really, he didn't know much about England. She was obviously homesick and without any substantial means, so that she could not return, at least until she had saved her fare. He felt a little sorry for her. What had brought her to his office, he asked. She didn't know, had just run her fingers down a list in the directory until she came to his name, and looked no further. It seemed fortuitous, he thought, that they should have immediately achieved such rapport – with what portent?

However he couldn't really prolong the visit; there was an afternoon's work to do. The tap-tap of the typewriter had ceased. Marilyn was possibly awaiting further assignments. He forced himself to bring the interview to a close.

'Well, Miss O. We must see how you get on. Let me know if you have any problems.'

He rose abruptly, as though in an effort to shake off what was obviously not his concern, and to resume his other work. She was a little taken aback at his change in manner.

'Yes,' she said, 'Thank you.'

She rose as though with a certain reluctance, but as she took up her bag, her expression, hitherto faintly wistful, changed to one of the same goodhumoured amusement he had seen when he made his entry. He saw her step past his desk. She did not take her eyes from his face until she had passed through the door, wearing the same twinkling gaze. He looked after her, and when she had gone remained standing, as though fixed to the spot. As he stood there, he heard Miss O.'s voice, seeming to come from the outer office. He went out. Miss O. stood at the counter.

'Mr French,' she said, 'I wanted to pay the account, I looked for your secretary, but there seems to be no-one here.'

'Oh,' he said, 'Oh,' realising suddenly that Marilyn had taken her lunch break. 'No,' he said, 'I'm sorry, my secretary has gone to lunch. Look,' he said impulsively, 'it was only a small matter. I won't make any charge.'

'But Mr French, I must pay my way. Will you send me an account?'

'No, Miss O. I won't send you an account for this. When you get established, come and see me then. It will be nice to see how well you are doing.' He hadn't any hopes for her in North Fremantle, and the remark. though encouraging, was hypocritical, but for some unaccountable reason, in a moment of self indulgence, he thought it would certainly be nice to see her again. Her face lit up.

'Oh, that's very nice of you. Thank you. Goodbye, then,' and without any further exchange, she had turned and was gone, walking away from him up the passage.

'I suppose I might as well have charged her,' he reflected gloomily, 'She won't do any good in North Fremantle, and someone else will get it.'

Nevertheless, he didn't feel bad about his minor generosity.

In the course of the following weeks, the incident naturally drifted to the back of his mind. He began to think of Miss O. at rare intervals, for he had ongoing matters to think of, to occupy his mind, as a pleasant memory, a little oddity among the multifarious collection of experiences of past encounters in his business, a curiosity, with her neat brown suit, and what he was somewhat rudely content to call her 'bashed-in hat'. It was a very appropriate, smart hat, really, in the fashion of the day, in as much as it included hats. They had ceased to be a regular item of apparel even in places of worship. Fashion and feminine aggrandisement were not always reconcilable in his mind. He was, as it happened, of a conservative persuasion, as befitted his vocation. Miss O. was, indeed, the epitome of his ideal of the mistress of a little tearoom. There was something quaintly old-fashioned about her. It was a wonder she had not gone into the business in Devon. If she did not make a success of it, it would not be her fault. He thought her attractive, but there was something about her which went further than attractiveness – he hadn't yet discovered what it was.

Jasper commuted to his business by train, a journey of about eleven minutes from boarding to alighting. Frequently, for one reason or another, he had to travel to Perth, and at such times his mind would be occupied with procedures, facts and innuendo because generally, it was to make an appearance in one or another of the courts of the capital, and he scarce found time to pay attention to what went on around him. On purely administrative matters, he would send Marilyn, who was more observant. On her return from one of these trips, quite unaccountably, Marilyn said to him: 'I saw Miss O. today.'

If she had said, 'I saw Sir Winston Churchill,' or, 'President Lyndon Johnston was at the Local Court, today,' her simple observation could not have had more impact.

'Miss O.!' he exclaimed, with unreasonable eagerness. It was an eagerness which he was too late to check. 'Who? – Oh, yes, Miss O.' He could not fail to perceive that his confusion was not lost on Marilyn, though he hastened to affect a milder interest, but he enquired, 'Where was she?'

'On the train, going to Perth.'

'Oh, really. Did you speak to her?'

'Yes, I was sitting next to her.'

'Well, well, what a coincidence! How is her business coming along?'

'I don't think she is working.'

'Hasn't she gone into business? She intended to open a tearoom.'

'I got the impression that she hadn't been able to go ahead with it.'

'Oh dear. What a shame. I wonder what has happened. I was interested in her.'

'Yes.'

'Professionally, of course. Professionally.'

'Of course.'

'Then of course, there was the possibility of being able to call in there on the way home, for a cup of tea.'

'Oh, sure.'

He made the remark to provoke the answer, but he didn't labour the point by saying that he didn't care for its tone, and simply went on:

'Where did she get on?'

'Just the other station past North Fremantle.'

'Well I never!'

It was futile for him to attempt to hide from Marilyn any personal interest in his former client. Marilyn was of an age when she was ultra-sensitive to atmospheres of this sort, and she was as sharp as a tack. It was galling but inescapable. He was more than vaguely interested, rather mysteriously. But why? It was disturbing. He'd only spoken to her for half an hour. He might have been twenty years her senior, but something about her had struck a chord. She was alone. She had the world at her feet, and was seeking a vocation, something to do with the rest of her life, perhaps. She had for a short spell been dependent on him for guidance and advice. It was as though she were his daughter. He entertained this concept for the briefest of moments, dismissing it shortly with some ve-hemence. Most certainly that was not how he felt. A normal reaction, perhaps, in view of the discussion which had followed the interview on a personal level. If she needed further assistance, he would consider her supplications on their merits. The opposite sex was no stranger to Jasper. He had had his experiences with its members, from time to time, some good, some bad. He prided himself that he had learned what there was to know. There was one thing for sure – they didn't pay his rent. One had to be a bit hard headed about them, take what was offered, treat them as human beings, and not get involved. The ability to disassociate himself from people was fostered by involvement in his profession. A lawyer cannot afford to get involved with his clients, or be swayed by their misfortunes. That was their business. His was to know the law, apply a considered interpretation of each person's connection with it, and for himself to make a living. With these summary philosophical reflections did Jasper attempt to dismiss from his mind the confusion which had surfaced in him when he was speaking to Marilyn, and turned his attention to things of a more practical nature.

A few days later he was himself travelling to Perth and returning by train about 1.00 p.m. The Fremantle bound and Perth bound services intersect at a station about half way between the termini, and the two trains waited briefly at that point. Suddenly he was attracted by the sight through the window of the compartment into that of the train about to move in the opposite direction. There, facing him, right before him in fact, at a distance of not more than ten feet, sat Miss O. She was quite lost in her own thoughts, her big grey eyes solemn. There was no way, short of making a complete fool of himself, that he could attract her attention. There was no point anyhow, since shortly they were to be speeding in opposite directions. Jasper could only look and accept the inevitable. It was unsettling thus to confront in person the subject which had been at the back of his mind for some weeks. It was almost as though she were tormenting him. The nature of the visit to his office had not been such as to warrant recording her address or telephone number. Even if it had he would not have felt justified in contacting her for personal reasons. He pondered the ethics of taking advantage of information confided in the course of a professional relationship, and glumly concluded that there was not in any event the possibility of that in the circumstances. All the same he was vastly unsettled by the encounter. Unaccountably, he found himself again wondering where she lived, why she had apparently not taken up a business, where she was going on these trains that enabled her so mysteriously to elude him, when he would have liked to know whether she had any problems, and if so, how he could help. He had enjoyed talking to her, and he wanted to see her again. He wanted to be a part of her action. The longer he was frustrated in this, the more insistent he felt about it. But it was quite obstinately not to be. 'We constantly,' he thought, 'remind ourselves that this is a small world, by observing coincidences of events and meetings at home and in far off places. Yet when we want to track down someone on our very doorsteps, the odds are stacked high against us.' He was again forced to accept that fate seemed to hold for him no such luck or particular favour, and in time drifted once more into philosophical acceptance of his lot. It was, after all, as no more than a dream which had passed in the night, leaving him wondering in the morning about the strangeness of things.

Jasper's life was, in the main, a selfish, insular existence. He dwelt within a small circle of acquaintances, on a standard which he did not have to struggle to maintain. He was fond of his comforts: he rarely took a holiday, but worked more or less continuously rather than hard. His work did not worry him, and he possessed the ability to forget it whilst outside his office. He was immediately resentful when, for one reason or another, it encroached on his leisure. He did not welcome work and was fortunate enough to be able to regard it as a necessary evil. It paid his way and enabled him to enjoy a reasonable level of ease. He had no one to please but himself. He was a man without love. Most of his clientele was ephemeral: some he chose to socialise with. While they provided him with a modicum of society, he became inwardly impatient when they made demands on his time and energy outside office hours. There was always the threat of an imposition on his good nature in an economic sense. He was reasonable with his charges for professional services, but occasionally took the liberty of frightening one of them off. He rarely regretted it. To some extent he enjoyed his work. He might as well, as it had to be done. The business was there, and it was a satisfaction to him to know that he was holding his own.

Miss O. was enthusiastic about her intention to commence a business, but she was young and inexperienced, and shortly discovered obstacles in her path. There was no shortage of rental accommodation in North Fremantle, but a paucity of suitable premises, and it soon became evident that what she wanted was very rare indeed. The owner of the shop she finally decided on was difficult to deal with. The rent he asked was exhorbitant; the conditions he imposed were unreasonable. Because she was a newcomer, he sought to take advantage of her lack of local knowledge, The prolixity of his demands was such that even Miss O. became suspicious. She asked him to set them all out in writing. She wanted a conclusive statement of conditions of occupation that he could not some time in the future vary to suit himself. What she was in fact seeking was a lease, though the concept had not crystallised in her mind. The owner declined to give any such statement, and reserved the right to change conditions. The result was a deadlock. After days of fruitless negotiating, Miss O. was utterly despondent. Though she lived frugally, her supply of money was depleting, and she was forced on to the labour market. She took a job as a waitress. It was casual but it enabled her better to form an idea of the condition of the industry, and what she might expect from it. She was able to ascertain as a result that her original ideas were somewhat idealistic. Service to the public in whatever capacity is always exacting, not always rewarding. Within the next few weeks she found, if she were not already aware of the fact, that it is advantageous always to be one step ahead of the customer. She learned to expect the worst whilst hoping for the best. Her spirit was not dampened; her energy and enthusiasm were not blunted, and her vision undimmed. Her employers were pleased with her. She worked at the 'El Caleb', which was an avant-garde coffee shop in East Perth, boasting foreign snacks and modern kitchen design and equipment ahead of the usual to be found in Perth Metropolitan District providers. She was honest and trustworthy and her services became invaluable. They saw the opportunity to open another shop. This necessitated putting Miss O. in full control of El Caleb. Their offer to her was impossible to refuse. It gave her the opportunity to be everything she had wanted, had she gone into business on her own account, without the responsibility of her own enterprise – without any responsibility save simply to account to her employers. The money wasn't bad. She even had days off within reason. For these she had to give notice of her intention so that suitable arrangements might be made for supervision during her absence. She vacated her accommodation, and took an apartment in East Perth. It was more expensive, but the saving in fares and travelling time made it worth while. There was reason to feel that she was on her feet, and at last, a step forward on the ladder of success.

In the course of these changes of lifestyle, some of the aspects of business which had crept into her interview with Jasper French assumed reality and she was reminded of her visit to his office. She smiled as she compared the trim cleanliness of her new surrounds with the dust and dishevelment of his untidy rooms. She recalled their meeting and the last encounter in the outer office. He had said she might come and see him again when she was in business. Well, here she was. He had never sent her an account. Perhaps she might discuss it with him now.

There was no earthly reason why Miss O. should call on Jasper in relation to his fee. He certainly did not expect her to. Something seemed to tell her that she must ring him. He had never given her any intimation that she owed him anything. Something seemed to motivate her insistently, like a kind of obsession. She was alone in Australia and, in time off from work, somewhat at a loss, at times, for diversion. Why had she come to Australia? She was really quite young. Was it the love of adventure? Was it a desire for relief from the grey skies of home? Was it the need to break free of the usual, the expected, the irksome ties of work, the prospects in her life? As she had sat in school in her middle teens, glancing momentarily from the window at the sometimes blue skies of Devon, while the stirrings of her girlhood built up inside her, she had become aware that those same blue skies ranged over other lands beside her own, somewhere there were boundless areas as yet unsettled, perhaps unexplored. A curious twinge of longing, of expectancy, of incompleteness assailed her. In the time which followed it never let her rest. In the ordinary course of things she left school, went to work, filled in her time as profitably as she could, until she was accepted for and underwent occupational training, while the idea crystallised in her mind. She delayed telling her parents until all arrangements were made. Those few who did know were incredulous. Certainly it had been a radical, a momentous decision, and she could never know how she made it. It was as though an unseen hand were guiding her in every move. Even the travel agents and Australian Immigration authorities were bewildered:

'I see, Miss O., by your application, that you've stated your destination as Perth. You'll be wanting to change that, I expect.'

'No, that's correct.'

'Perth! You want to go to Perth. There's nothing there. It's only a backwater, you know. We'll put you down for Sydney.'

'I don't want to go to Sydney. I want to go to Perth.'

'You won't like it. There's no work there. You won't stay five minutes when you find what it's like. Well, what about Melbourne, then, if you don't want to go to Sydney?'

'No, I want to go to Perth.'

'Why Perth? For heaven's sake. Have you any relations there?'

'No.'

'Friends?'

'No.'

'But you want to go to Perth?'

'Yes.'

'Oh, very well then, Perth it is, if that's what you say.'

Why Perth indeed? But in any event, why not? If the truth were known, and certainly the truth was a stranger to her, though she felt it, there was always the hint of an extra compulsion in every move she made, a little force which had the effect of surprising even her at times, small but determined, a tiny angel of omniscience ranged over her side in this tremendous foray into the unknown. Well, now she had come to Australia, she was certainly homesick, and would have given a lot to be back again at home; but she nevertheless could not disabuse her mind of the notion that she had been sent for a purpose. She had no idea what that purpose might be. She had made a few acquaintances, but none whom she could call friend. She lived a very isolated life. Jasper was one person, at least, with whom she had struck a common chord. They had talked of things of which both had an intimate knowledge, on a plane which revealed a mutual sensitivity. If you had asked her at that moment why it was that she had an impulse to discuss with Jasper their financial relationship, she would likely have been unable, and at best unwilling, to tell you the truth. The opportunity presented itself when she had a little time to spare, and she telephoned his office. Marilyn answered the call, and Mr French was out, she said. Could she have a number to return the call? Well, no, but perhaps Marilyn could inform her when it would be most convenient to Mr French, for her to call him again.

Suddenly, Marilyn's voice became more excited. 'Oh!' she said, 'Mr French has just come in; if you will hold the line, I will ask him if he will speak to you.'

At that moment, in his customary inconsequentiality, Jasper had entered the office. The information thus unexpectedly imparted took Miss O. by surprise. She had not been confident of a welcoming reception by Jasper, and she had not been entirely prepared for the line she must take on that account to justify her call. It had been almost with a sense of relief that she had discovered that he was out. Now she had again to marshal her thoughts.

As he approached her desk, Marilyn said, 'Mr French, it's Miss O. speaking.'

He stopped, dumbfounded, then, 'Put her through to my office,' he said shortly, and went through the door. He lifted the handpiece, and after a moment's hesitation, 'French speaking,' he volunteered in his best manner.

He represented himself on the telephone as being deeply interested in Miss O.'s story of the forced abandonment of her original idea, her progress and her change of address. He expressed approval and pleasure at what she had accomplished. He firmly and resolutely declined to make any charge to her whatever, claiming that their agreement had been that he would do so when she was successfully in her own business. They discussed her future plans. He ascertained that she was still homesick, still cherished the idea of going back to Britain, but was uncertain as to how and when that might be accomplished. She was obviously very pleased with her progress, however; she was more secure, more confident. Her occupation was satisfactory. There was still something amiss. They remained in conversation for fifteen minutes, and Marilyn was eventually obliged to interrupt by saying that a certain Mr X. was in the waiting area, asking if Mr French could see him. Jasper was obliged to bring the conversation to a close.

'So it's East Perth, where you're working, El Caleb?

'Yes, Mr French.'

'Well, first opportunity I get, I'd like to call in.'

'I can promise you good service.'

'Great. I have to go now, if you will excuse me. Perhaps I'll see you soon.'

'Yes, I'll look forward to it,' and she hung up.

Jasper was eminently pleased with the information imparted in this exchange. At last, he thought, there was some resolution of the questions which had been at the back of his mind for some weeks. He was content, now, to let things work themselves out, and he made no special arrangements to visit Perth. He was content to savour the anticipation of a meeting with Miss O. until it should transpire in the ordinary course of events, and even when he had a momentary opportunity, he did not seize it, but waited until he could call at El Caleb at his leisure. He wanted to have time to talk. The chance arose on a Wednesday afternoon when the lunch time business had slackened at the café. They were able to renew their acquaintanceship with a minimum of interruption.

It was in the weeks that followed that Jasper became a regular customer at El Caleb, and he anticipated his visits with increasing pleasure as he and Miss O. came better to know each other. Part of his practice was centred on a country town, where he had a longer association with farmers and business in and within a large radius. A magistrate held court in the town once a month, and Jasper made a point of visiting on that day, sometimes involved in litigation, and in any event, in the pursuit of further business. Over the years, with changes in personnel and structure, the association had decreased in importance as his Fremantle practice grew. He no longer regarded it as a vital adjunct to his office work, and now treated the visit as something of a vacation, a welcome break from city routine. If he was not engaged in court proceedings, he would renew old acquaintances, reassure clients of his continued existence, see and be seen in the town. He had spoken of his country visits to Miss O. On a day when he was taking coffee with her, he was suddenly struck with a bright idea. It was a flash of inspiration.

He said: 'I have to go to the country again on Wednesday week. I wonder, Miss O., if you would consider coming with me. I have to be away overnight, putting up at a local hotel, and back next day. It would be a change for you. I'd have the benefit of your company, and you'd see a bit of the countryside. Are you interested?'

To his absolute incredulity, her answer came after only the briefest of pauses. 'Yes, Mr French. I think I'd like that. I'll try to get some time off.'

'Fine,' he said, 'I'll ring you at the restaurant and confirm the arrangements. It will be Perth Central Railway station at 4 p.m. on Wednesday the 16th.'

'Thank you, Mr French,' she said simply. 'I'll look forward to it.'

He couldn't really have believed that his offer would be accepted. It was a shot in complete darkness. She had not argued or imposed conditions. He knew her well enough to know that she was not naive about it. She must trust him implicitly. He felt strangely flattered. He certainly refused to think of the expedition as other than a pleasurable jaunt, or of his prospective companion as other than someone to talk to on the journey. It was a definite improvement on talking to strangers, or having no one to talk to at all. It would, he reflected, be a bit like taking a little girl for a walk in the park, enjoying the child's reactions on seeing the trees and the flowers; but with the added attraction of the responses of a young adult.

Miss O. was outwardly and quietly pleased to see Jasper, arriving after him at Central Station, and after their mutual greeting, they together boarded the little diesel car. The middle of the week drew few passengers. He was elated to receive his companion. She was arrayed in a machine knitted, light woollen navy blue suit with slim white edging about the neck and cuffs and the hem of the skirt. There was nothing special about her attire, he noted, remembering the rather ordinary suit she had worn on the day of their first meeting, but she carried herself with a dignity mysteriously combined in her appearance with the freshness and vivacity of youth, such that he was oblivious to any lack of distinction in her apparel. He had the impression that she would have looked rather stunning whatever she wore, and certainly she shone among all others on the platform like a single dewdrop glinting in the sun. She carried a small suitcase with her handbag. He took it from her and shepherded her aboard. They took their seats opposite each other in a carriage with few passengers. He looked at her with slight embarrassment. It was incumbent on him, he was thinking, carefully to consider his real motives in bringing this young person away from her home, into hired lodgings overnight, anonymously, among strangers. If she was not naive, she knew what she was doing. It was appropriate then to be friendly, polite and attentive. Indeed, at no time did he wish to be anything else. He thought she was beautiful, but in truth it was not so much aesthetic perfection as the friendly familiarity which she exuded with such paradoxically tantalising remoteness. He was forcibly and irresistibly reminded of the role which had suggested itself to him in the confusion which had arisen in his mind in the aftermath of their first meeting. He was her senior, he had made a place for himself in the world, and she was still as driftwood, unestablished. She needed his friendship, his guidance, his trustworthiness. He was determined that these should not be lacking.

His enthusiasm knew no bounds, however. 'Who would have thought you would have been travelling with me?' he exclaimed. 'I do hope the trip will be to your liking.'

'Well, I've certainly nothing better to do,' she answered with a bright smile. She was as bemused with the situation as he. 'I haven't been anywhere for ages, let alone this kind of outing. I think it will be very interesting.'

She had made acquaintances, but no friends as yet, and certainly none to whom she could cleave for support, or on whom rely for companionship. If the truth were known, she was apt to make staunch friends, but was selective in her choice. She displayed a lively interest in the scenery: the countryside, always a source of enjoyment to Jasper, came to teem with fresh delight, as he described the sights and the kinds of lives the rural people led, punctuating his account with anecdotes which occurred to him from time to time. He commenced to talk to relieve his own self consciousness, but it was soon apparent that he had plunged into a sea of reminiscence, to which she gave all appearance of being an ardent and amused listener. Her interest impelled him into further excesses, in which he quite forgot himself, though it could be gathered that he talked about himself a good deal. Out from the commercial and industrial suburbs east of Perth, the train commenced its ascent of the ranges with the sun still warm on the windows, and the colours of the vegetation were decisive in the clear light of the autumn afternoon. He spoke of the transformation which would take place after the first rains, and hoped she would come again with him in the winter, when the valley of the river would be softened with green, and the river itself swollen from a trickle to a flood. He eulogised about the orange groves and orchards that the area could sustain, the hill slopes, the quaint towns, the crops that could be grown, and the red earth turned by the plough.

It was an hour before he drew rein, realising at last that his patient audience might need a cup of tea, and some respite. She responded prettily to his invitation.

'You stay here,' he said, 'and I'll bring it to you. Would you like something to eat? We can, I think, get dinner of a sort.'

He re-emerged in a few minutes from the refreshment car, bearing a tray. The train resumed after a brief stop, and they bent over their plates together. She thanked him warmly. By the time they had finished their meal darkness had fallen. The shadows had lengthened in the last vestiges of golden sunshine, until they eventually dissolved in a twilight so short as to be forgotten almost immediately. No longer was there scenery for discussion, and the couple were thrown on their own resources.

Throughout Jasper maintained a polite but studious avoidance of undue familiarity.

His efforts to do so were placed under severe strain when his companion drew his attention to a column she had observed in the evening newspaper. He leant forward to read it where it lay on her knee. Their heads touched unexpectedly, and he felt the soft curl of her hair against his temple. It was an innocent accidental contact, but quite cataclysmic for them both, and he withdrew sharply with a strange feeling as though he had been caught out in a guilty act. It was a few moments before he regained his sangfroid, and he could not help feeling that she had been similarly affected. He deemed it tactful to make no reference to the incident, but was unable somehow to dismiss it from his mind.

At length they arrived at their destination, and together stepped into the clear night air. There was no moon, and in the station yard before the street lighting, the starlight pierced the darkness with white intensity. Then they came upon their hotel. Jasper secured two single rooms at some distance from each other. He bade his fellow traveller goodnight, hoped she had had a satisfactory journey, and that he would see her at breakfast. She replied to his salutations with unassuming friendliness.

'It has been lovely. So nice to have someone to talk to on a personal level. I haven't enjoyed myself so much since I arrived in Australia.'

She was obviously sincere; there were no inhibitions. He was relieved of any embarrassment, and thought the invitation was there to suggest that they should while away another hour over a cup of tea. But the bar was closed and the hour was late. Country folk do not favour the idea of late hours, and it was unlikely that there would be a café or tearooms to afford them the excuse to stay up. In any event he was never sure what he might be called on for the morrow. She, of course, had nothing to occupy her while he was engaged, however long that might be. 'I hope you won't find tomorrow too dull. I'll try to be finished early,' he said, 'so that we can look around before the train leaves – er, if you haven't already done so.'

'What time is that?'

'Four-thirty p.m.'

'Shall I see you at breakfast?'

'Yes, 7.30.'

'Oh, good.'

'Well, goodnight.'

'Thank you, Mr French. Goodnight.'

The exchange took place outside the room he had booked for her, and he turned to proceed to his. When he arrived at his door, he saw her still standing in the passage outside her room. It seemed to be getting more and more difficult to remain informal.

Jasper was elated with his suggestion for the trip and its success. He was full of enthusiasm for his new friend. He sidestepped the notion that he was getting into deep water. The strange encounter on the train was worrying, and persistent. With anyone with whom he had ever become involved he could not recall that he had ever felt as he had then. He felt rather like a boy caught in a forbidden situation he had secretly enjoyed. He couldn't communicate his feelings to his companion; it would probably be an embarrassment to her to refer to it. He had noted the colouring of her cheeks and the aversion of her eyes, and he had been pushed to the brink of utterance on the subject; but some things were better left unsaid. He took stock of his position. If he had been younger, it might have been reasonable to declare his position, his feelings. What were they? He was, he had eventually to admit, falling in love with her. He realised he must have been in love ever since their first encounter, and had never admitted it to himself: that was evidently the reason that he now found himself in this precarious predicament. He knew that nothing could come of it. For what was he doing with a girl so much younger? And what could she see in a man old enough to be – he refused to pursue the matter any further. He pondered that she still wanted to go back to England, and was homesick. Presumably, she would, in time, save enough money for her fare, and be able to travel in comfort. Perhaps she would allow him to help her; that would let her have her way sooner, and, at the same time, end the impossible situation into which they were surely drifting. He thought about it carefully, and at length conceived a plan of action. He vowed to put the matter to her at breakfast.

But the morning came, and when he went downstairs to the dining room, he found her full of anticipation for the day ahead, and it seemed incongruous to broach the subject which had consumed his attention throughout the night's waking moments. He was unwilling to spoil her fun. She greeted him with enthusiasm, and the customary pleasantries followed.

'Have you any plans for the day?' he asked.

'Well, I'll just get my bearings, look at the shops and town generally, have a cup of tea. I don't know how long that will take.'

'Not long, I expect. I'll look out for you when I'm free, and perhaps we can have lunch together.'

'Oh. lovely, but don't worry about me. What time must we be at the station?'

He hadn't told her that he usually caught a lift in a commercial car up from the city, which returned at 4 p.m. He suggested it to her now. Privately, he thought it a safer course than to risk a possible recurrence of any familiarity on the train.

'Oh, that will be a nice change. Will the driver take an extra passenger?'

'I'm sure he will. He more or less expects to backload on the return journey. I expect to be through this morning,' he added, 'and perhaps I could meet you at one for a spot of lunch.'

Jasper was perfectly prepared to modify his habit of avoiding lunch to suit his charming companion. They met at the hotel, but decided instead of lunch to take tea and sandwiches at a street café. It was a day of the livestock sales, and the shop was well patronised and noisy with farmers' agents, locals and workmen, some with wives, or otherwise unattached members of the opposite sex, all looking for casual refreshment, and the staff was kept busy with orders for tables and take-away fare, to the extent that service was noticeably slow. They were jostled going in and coming out, and they were obliged to share a table with strangers. Conversation was not possible in any depth, but Miss O. appeared to be intrigued with the sights and sounds. Since he had no special engagements for the afternoon, they lingered over the table until the customers thinned out and the noise of many voices and the clatter of dishes had died down. It was pleasant to sit and enjoy each other's company. He found himself wishing that it did not have to end, whether they talked or not. It was with some difficulty that he proposed his plan – a plan which would spell the doom of their association.

'I've no doubt that you'd be glad to be in England with your own people.'

'Yes indeed,' she answered.

He felt he had the opportunity he needed. 'I have an idea. Shall I tell you about it?'

'Oh, yes.'

'I would have no difficulty in opening an overdraft account,' he said, 'with a limit, say, of whatever would be sufficient to see you safely home – your fare, by ship or air if you prefer, with enough to meet train, taxi and incidental expenses. I would give the bank authority to meet all cheques drawn on a cheque book which you will operate up to that limit. Then when you get work, you can repay the bank what you have used. There will be interest, but the rate is quite reasonable at present, and will probably not inconvenience you.'

'Mr French, that is a wonderful idea, and it would be simply great.' She spoke with warmth. But then her face fell, and she shook her head . . . 'But I simply could not accept it.'

'Why not? It's all strictly business, and I'm not making anything out of it. It's just as though I were a guarantor really, and I know you well enough to feel safe in the knowledge that it's not costing me anything.'

'Oh, I would see to that,' she assured him.

'Well, it's settled then; shall I make the arrangements?'

She was silent for a moment, then, 'I suppose so,' she said.

It was an idyllic afternoon. They left the little café, and walked eastwards down the main street of the town. The flurry and excitement of the sales were waning now. Motorists, mainly farmers, were loading provisions into their vehicles. It was May, autumn was nearly over and a light rain was forecast, enough to spur the farmers into active preparations for cultivating the soil and planting crops. There was no time for them to socialise. Seed had to be prepared, fertilizer carted, machinery cleaned and oiled and stock organised into appropriate paddocks for agistment and protection against the ravages of winter. The activity in the town would abate in the warm sun of the afternoon. The couple had not far to walk to be out of town altogether. Silence fell between them. There seemed to be nothing to say. Conversation seemed to be not only difficult, but also entirely unnecessary. It was clear, however, that if they were to catch the lift, they must keep it in mind, and Jasper said they had better be getting back. Reluctantly, but with more haste now, they returned to the hotel, picked up their bags and presented themselves to the driver. At 4 p.m. sharp, they drove off, and at 8 p.m. Miss O. was dropped in East Perth.

They were back in their respective routines, and Jasper took a suburban train home.

He proceeded to make the necessary arrangements with his bank to finance Miss O.'s return to England, without delay. He rejected consideration of any further or closer association with her. In due course the bank informed him that his overdraft had been approved. It was time to contact her and say that the finance was available. He thought he could allow himself a small indulgence. There was less risk of involvement now, nothing could come of it. He telephoned her at the restaurant.

'El Caleb. Miss O. speaking.'

'Miss O. This is Jasper French. How are you?'

'Oh, Mr French. How nice to hear from you. I'm very well, thank you.'

'Miss O., I'm taking the liberty to ask you if you would be interested in having dinner with me one evening. What do you say?'

'Oh yes, that would be lovely.'

'What evening are you free?'

'I haven't any engagements. Any evening would do.'

He had expected something of the sort. He said, 'Later this week, Friday – shall we make it 7.00 p.m.?'

'Oh, yes, certainly.'

'Right, I'll call for you then.' She confirmed her address with him and rang off.

It was five weeks since he had spoken to her, and he might well have believed she had forgotten all about him and the arrangement he had proposed.

She had not.

Her enthusiasm was infectious, and he looked forward to Friday evening with a delicious sense of alarm. However, he anticipated the delight on her face when he would tell her his news. How pleased she would be – wouldn't she? To be going home after all these months of loneliness and homesickness. It was true she had a good position, and was comfortably rewarded financially; but she could look forward to a couple of years of this before she could afford a return fare. She had her work, no friends, few acquaintances and little society of any kind. Evidently she regarded her return as a priority, ruling out other personal enjoyment. He took pleasure in a generous act in which he found a good deal of personal satisfaction. He subdued a feeling of dismay in knowing that he might soon see the last of her. He tried to persuade himself that it was not his business.

There are some benefits in running one's own business. He scheduled his work to give him release from the office at 4 p.m. on Friday. He did not want to be hurried in getting home, changing and travelling to keep his appointment. He took a taxi from Perth and arrived at the East Perth address a few minutes after seven. Miss O. opened to his knock. She was obviously prepared and appeared radiant.

'I have a taxi waiting,' he greeted.

They boarded the cab and the driver speeded to a prearranged destination, where they moved indoors and were ushered to a table. It was dimly lit and pervaded by a pleasing background music. In between ordering drinks and courses, a general conversation ensued, chiefly about the food and the restaurant, and the importance of making a wise choice of venue, the industry being very much in its infancy in West Australia. Jasper had not spoken to Miss O. since their venture into the country save to make these arrangements. He had not been in any hurry to convey to her the results of the finance application, although the bank had given its approval a fortnight before. The matter could not be postponed indefinitely, and he braced himself to come to the point. They were awaiting dessert when he said;

'Now to get down to business.'

She looked at him enquiringly.

He did not return her look. He was fumbling with the tableware. He had some difficulty in going on. He didn't want to show his embarrassment, and in an effort to appear as cool as possible, but without conviction, he approached the subject in a very different way from that which he had intended. Some sub-conscious force was operating to delay the announcement he knew he was obliged to make. If he had had to inform her that the bank had turned down his application, he would have found it easier. After a minute's delay, he gathered himself together and said quite miserably:

'I've arranged an overdraft. You have to sign this paper, and I authorise your signature. Then you take it to the bank and are issued with a cheque book. So you are now free to make your arrangements to go back to England whenever you like.'

He gave her the account form to sign and she looked at it. He said, 'I suppose you'll want to move fairly promptly now.'

She flushed slightly and looked away. He thought she had never looked so lovely. Her face had assumed an archness tinged with a faint embarrassment. She had been anticipating this scene, this climax, this termination of their friendship. and had been unable to conceive a plan to deal with it. He had made no declaration, though she felt certain that the end was as repugnant to him as to her. She was on a spot. All her womanly instincts rebelled against the decision she must take; and that was capitulation, pure and simple. He had, unwittingly enough, it is true, manipulated her into a position in which she must, however indirectly, declare her true feelings. It was inevitable, it was undignified, demoralising, but it was worth it. He had no concept of the tumult going on within her, He was fully expecting her to welcome the chance that was offered to her, and take early advantage of it. He looked at her expectantly, waiting for the signs of pleasure and anticipation which must surely come. They didn't. Instead she said:

'I'm not going back to England now.'

He looked at her in amazement. He was bereft of speech.

'You're not – you're not go –' he couldn't get any more out. His mind had gone blank, and he could only wait on her further explanation.

'I want to stay here,' she said. She had been unable to look him straight in the eye, but when she said this her face assumed more solemnity, and she gazed at him steadfastly. He began to comprehend. He reached out a hand and took hers. The same thrill coursed through his as on other occasions when they had made contact. What was the use? He was in love with her.

He said, 'I'm in love with you.'

'I know,' she answered, and a great sense of relief settled over them both.

And the little spirit, which had so expectantly, so assiduously, and so anxiously hovered over them both for so long, suddenly executed a pirouette in a transport of sheer delight.

Christmas Eve

In the darkness I lie thinking,
Listen for the Sleigh bells clinking,
Try to stop myself from blinking,
Into dreamland slowly sinking

Santa Claus! Is that you on the stairs?

Up the wooded hillsides steep there,
In fields past idly grazing sheep there,
On ships tossed on the ocean deep there,
Through cities where folk lie asleep there –

Santa Claus! Is that you on the stairs?

In the spangled wake he traces,
Dreaming in their distant places,
Lie the children's happy faces,
Locked in slumber's fast embraces –

Santa Claus! Is that you on the stairs?

Oh! The glory of the morning,
'Neath the shelter of love's awning,
Seeds of joy and goodwill spawning –
Faith rekindled, freshly dawning –

That was Santa I heard on the stairs!

A Breath Of Country Air

Mary Sutton pursed her lips. She lay very comfortably on some generous cushions spread along a cane lounge beneath the grapevines climbing over the pergola in her garden. It was a warmish day and she luxuriated in a situation of her own attainment. She was not a plain woman, and her youthful face was enhanced by a sharpness of intellect and a predilection to humour. Her figure was nothing if not voluptuous, so that the gaps between the cushions were compensated for by the generosity of her proportions, exhibiting a predisposition to relaxation and disinclination to exertion. When the occasion demanded, as it perpetually did, she carried out her household chores and the care of her family with a judicious mixture of stoicism and responsibility which left no room for criticism. But she loved her ease as well, and neglected no opportunity to indulge herself in those delights to which every woman earns the right: a little indolence, a little peace, another woman to talk to of fashion, of cuisine, of other women, in short a little gossip. The balmy atmosphere of her back garden, typical of the time of the year throughout the south-west, encouraged in her a mood of somnolence, disturbed only at this time by the inescapable knowledge that her son David was leaving home that day for the first time and going to the country. He was eighteen, and had got a job with a shearing team. He was to be a rouseabout. Weekends, perhaps, while the team was not too far from the city, and probably during crutching, he might be home. After that, he might be away six months at a time. There is usually an anxious feeling on the part of the mother, if not also on that of the child, at the first separation, and its presence was not masked on this occasion by Mary's pseudo sophistication. In fact it was heightened by the certain knowledge that David had received a summons issued by a country District Police Court requiring him to attend Petty Sessions on a charge of speeding. It seemed that on a recent visit to Merredin to be interviewed for the job, he had been in a hurry to return with a story of success, and the news had been dampened rather by the outcome of his over-enthusiasm. He was a well set up youth, with athletic build, brown arms and face and regular features, of average height, not taller than his father who was also a shearer, and endowed with some of his mother's charm. He had no particular education, and was content to follow in the footsteps of his father, who was a shearing contractor. Mary was pleased that he should have become a man who accepted his place in life without question; he had qualities of leadership, she thought, and could manage a team just as his father had, perhaps better. After all, she had had a hand in his making. He sat now, in front of his mother, disconsolate, at a loss for conversation. There was this question of the speeding charge. She looked at him.

'You'll lose your licence, for sure,' she worried, 'and you've only just got it, you might say.'

In fact, his probation had expired, since he had, with the inveterate haste of young motorist hopefuls, secured his P-plates within a couple of weeks of his seventeenth birthday. Nevertheless, he was unable to counter his mother's discouraging avowal.

'You had better see Jasper about it,' his mother went on. 'He attends the court there. He's always very helpful to me, and I'm sure he'd do what he can for you.'

Jasper French was a lawyer who lived in close proximity. He practised in Fremantle but visited Merredin on a monthly basis to coincide with the Magistrate's visit to that town. It was a long trip which took him from his Fremantle practice to its detriment at times, but it offered the opportunity and provided the excuse to break from city routine. He travelled to and from by train, a service which conveniently matched his needs for transport. When he stepped aboard at Fremantle, it was like entering a new world, and he had the sensation of being freed from the cares of the office for a day at least. The train carried him during the late afternoon hours through the hills of the Darling Escarpment into the fertile farming districts of Muresk, Toodyay and Northam. He had been up and down the line all his life, it seemed to him, but the sight of the green orchards, maturing cereal crops and chocolate fallow soil, interspersed with woodland, never ceased to impress him with that other side of life, so different from the one which he had chosen, in which people tilled the earth and tended the herd: the useful, productive people who had little use for books, rules and regulations, and whose industry never failed to make him feel a little guilty in his legal academia. He had a keen eye for the wild duck flying north in the autumn, the green velvet of the grass springing up in the first rain, the winter turmoil of storm, flood and hail, the first fresh burst of spring sunshine and the multifarious activities of animal, bird and insect. He regretted the litigation which of necessity at times weaned his mind from all these delights, but he enjoyed talking to the countryfolk on non-litigious business. He had previously practised in Merredin and was loath to abandon his country clientele. He was on good terms with the local police and the court personnel.

'You will probably see him at the Court,' Mary persisted. She was anxious in her protective maternal role for her son's sake that reasonable steps should be taken to shield him from unnecessary punitive action. 'Unless you want to give him a call now?' questioningly. But with the casual intransigence of youth, David did not contact the lawyer.

A glance at the court list of business required to be dealt with by the Magistrate on his periodical visit to hold court in a country place will be sufficient to reveal the detail and variety of matters involved. Traffic administration and control, owing to the ubiquitous motor car, demand a large proportion of the court's time, and it may be forgiven, therefore, if it should play a prominent role in this report. But it so happened that about the time when Mrs Sutton's young aspirant had been exposed in a surreptitious breach of proper conduct, another gentleman of the road fell into disrepute in the same vicinity. He was a pastoralist from a sheep station in the open country well beyond Merredin. He had been to Perth to purchase a new FWD utility, and through circumstances beyond his control, was obliged to drive it back home on his own. It was a journey of a thousand kilometres. He had made it before on a number of occasions, and the prospect of doing it again did not appeal. After he had driven through the hills and reached the flat country, the sameness of the experience started to pall, and he was at a loss as to how to combat the ennui. The radio was poor company. Reception was bad anyway, and the country transmitters did not provide entertainment to his taste. It was difficult to devise a diversion while keeping his mind on the road and maintaining a viable speed. About a hundred miles out of

Perth he stopped for a drink. It was 8 p.m.; there were in the bar of this country tavern a couple of loafers and an aboriginal man, all of whom had drunk too much to provide him with any entertainment. Fluorescent lighting emphasised the shabbiness and the worst aspects of the interior. He bought a bottle of Teacher's Highland Cream and went back to his vehicle. He took a swig.

The whisky gave him a lift, and reminded him at the same time that he had not had anything to eat since lunch. Certainly he needed some refreshment. He took another swig.

For some reason it did not occur to him to seek out solid refreshment in the village, and he drove on in obvious enjoyment of what he was imbibing. He was drinking the whisky direct from the bottle, steering with his left hand whilst he held it to his lips with his right. It went down fine. It was a pleasant balmy evening, with no sound save the mutter of the engine and the brilliance of the stars for company. The sky was an all-enveloping canopy of navy velvet. By the time he had reached the outskirts of Merredin the 750 millilitre bottle was more than three quarters gone. He was elated.

But the liquor was having its effect. As he passed the street which runs south from the rail station in the town's centre, he was having difficulty staying on the road. It came to him momentarily that there was a steering fault in this new vehicle. It traced a crazy path. He had slowed its speed to accommodate its eccentricities, but even this was not sufficient to keep it on track; finally the left front wheel ran over the edge. He could not, did not, try to bring it back. The vehicle went down until the soft loose gravel shoulder of the road caught the sump. The motor coughed a couple of times and gave up. Freed from the onerous duty of steering any longer, the driver dropped an empty bottle, leaned across the wheel and fell asleep. Quiet reigned.

'We've got a client for you!' were among the first words which greeted Jasper when he sauntered into the police station on his next Merredin visit. They were not so much his friends as business associates. He invariably called in to see them whether he had any business with them or not, and they seemed pleased to see him, or at least they expected him. He regarded it as a necessary and not unpleasant routine. In the winter, the country was cold and dry, for the most part; rain was generally all too seldom an element to be reckoned with. A light wind from the east was sufficient to make mugs of hot coffee welcome to hold in the hands and consume these cold mornings, while discussing local news and, perhaps, even business. Sometimes, Jasper was involved in disputes which might engage all his attention, and then he was preoccupied and busy, interviewing witnesses, studying documents, conferring with opponents. Sometimes the police were his opponents. This morning he was employed on a number of non-litigious matters, none of which was sufficient to absorb him entirely, and – yes, he was most interested in the somewhat unusual circumstances which made it possible for the police to say that they had a client for him.

Sergeant Starr was a big man by anybody's standards. He was officer in charge, and his able and popular assistant was Constable Carmelo (Charlie) Parenino. The Constable was familiarly known to Jasper by the English derivation of his first name, as was Douglas Starr to the farmers and townsfolk among whom he moved. Somehow or other, Jasper always felt the necessity to address the Sergeant by his rank, or at least a diminutive of it. There was that about the Sarge which always commanded his respect. His size was daunting enough, but there was a precision in all his movements, an obvious mastery of himself, which set him apart as a leader. Jasper would have hated to be on the wrong side of him. Anyway, he liked, admired, and respected him.

'What's that? A client? How? Who?' He did not comprehend.

The Sergeant gave an account of the events of the evening when they had found an insensible man in his utility in the ditch off the Highway, and the information derived from the man's statement to him about the circumstances which had brought him there. He and the Constable had brought him into the lock-up, bedded him down, given him breakfast, facilitated his toilet arrangements, charged him and subsequently sent him on his way.

'If we had brought him before the Court in the morning,' he said, 'of course, you know, there would have been Js. P. on the bench, and he would have lost his licence there and then. So after we charged him, we gave him back his keys so that he could drive home. He had about eight hundred kilometres to go, and if he couldn't drive he'd have no way of getting there.'

Well, that was human anyway, and plain common sense, thought Jasper. 'For sure,' he said, 'he could have still been there. There's no transport out in that part of the world. But –' His mind was already engaged with questions of defence, proper instructions, lawyer–client relationship, professional procedures, costs. True, he had no reason to doubt the Sergeant's integrity. He had already done the man a good turn by releasing the vehicle keys to him. From what he had been told of the driver's escapade, there was obviously no defence. Could Jasper be sure of this? He thought he could. The Sergeant had allowed the charge to stand over for nearly a month before bringing it before the Court, telling the defendant of the expected visit of the lawyer and the opportunity of securing his services, when the charge would be read, if he were agreeable. It was unlikely that Jasper would be able to contact his 'client' before the charge was read. It would seem, moreover, that the Sergeant was motivated as much by a willingness to do a good turn to the persons with whom he was dealing as by any other reason. Jasper decided that he could accept the assignment.

'What's his name?' he asked.

'Jim French. J. S. French of Barlee Station,' was the reply. The man had the same surname and initials as his proposed representative. 'Your namesake. A good bloke, he is. Just got a bit bored travelling back from Perth, and called in for a bit of refreshment down the track. We had to put him in overnight.'

'And he's charged with driving under the influence?'

'Yes; he wants you to front for him.'

'He wants me to plead guilty for him, does he?' Jasper didn't want any doubts to arise.

'That's about the size of it. He's got no defence. He'll have a conviction, and'll lose his licence for three months. It's a first offence. He'll be able to cut that time out on the station up there.'

'Very convenient, I must say. Don't suppose he comes down this road very often.'

The die was cast. The busy little court was abuzz with voices as Jasper walked in the main door. Suiters had been attracted from towns and farming properties for miles around. A few curious glances were cast in his direction, some to find out what the visiting lawyer looked like, some to ascertain what a lawyer was, having never previously seen one. Litigants, defendants, witnesses and onlookers jostled for space, and clerks fussed in and out of the side doors leading to the offices and the magistrate's chambers, as they gave final touches to the arrangements for hearing. Jasper approached the desk, and locating the name of his client, he pointed it out to the clerk who was bending over the list.

'Plea of guilty,' he said; the clerk nodded without looking up.

'I'll call it first up,' he said, and jotted the information down beside the name.

'Oh! Good,' Jasper replied and walked back to take up his position at the bar table.

In a few minutes a court orderly called out 'Order in the Court!' The buzz of voices was stilled, and as it subsided, the magistrate emerged from his side entrance at the rear of the dais; he was a small, unassuming man, with a mop of grey hair smoothed into a modest and unremarkable style. His suit was grey, his tie was grey, his face not appreciably other than grey. It was with quiet dignity, almost boredom, that he took his seat, and there descended upon the court an atmosphere of quiet expectancy, whilst the orderly announced in commanding tones: 'Court of Petty Sessions now in session. Traffic Court case Number 7 on the list – J. S. French.'

The clerk handed up a file to the Magistrate, who looked it over and cast his eyes expectantly at the bar. Jasper had risen to his feet. He was a familiar sight to the magistrate. 'If it please the court,' he announced, 'I appear for the accused.'

'Yes, Mr French, I'll read the charge – The accused is charged in that on the – – – day of – – – 19 – – at Merredin, he drove a vehicle, to wit, a – – – –, registered number – – – – on a road, namely, Great Eastern Highway, whilst under the influence of alcohol to such an extent as to be incapable of having proper control thereof. Do you plead guilty or not guilty?'

'If you please, Sir, the accused pleads guilty.'

'Thank you, Mr French. What are the facts, Sergeant?'

Sergeant Starr rose, towering above the bar table, so that he was obliged to stoop to gain or regain hold of his papers. He gave an unadorned account of the events leading up to the arrest of the station owner, and sat down.

'Thank you, Sergeant. Anything to say, Mr French?'

'There are no extenuating circumstances, Sir.' In any event the nature of the charge does not admit of any amelioration of the penalty, and besides Jasper did not want to provoke the Magistrate into any remarks concerning his client's conduct, which, he was perfectly aware, was, to say the least, somewhat carefree.

'Thank you. Any record, Sergeant?' The Magistrate continued without embellishment.

'No record, Sir,' was the reply.

Sentence was pronounced, and the orderly called the next charge. It was as simple as that. The audience remained silent as if with awe at the majesty of justice.

'Well,' thought Jasper, as he gathered his few things and walked from the Court, 'I suppose it's all grist for the mill.' He had sundry other appearances to make during the session, and then turned his attention to office work and socialising. It had become a very pleasant day without blemish. He sought out the address and telephone number of his client from Barlee Station, and telephoned and spoke to a woman who answered his call. Mr French was eight miles away fixing a windmill on a soak well. Jasper left his own particulars, with an invitation to return the call. He did not expect to hear from him. Country people are notoriously slack in matters of business, even of law, he was well aware. He turned his attention to other things. The little town was busy with the influx of farmers and buyers to the livestock sales, and the streets were in festive mood. It was a good day for business and pleasure alike. Warm sunshine now complemented the bustle and chatter in the dusty main street. The grocers, teashops and taverns were doing a brisk trade; countless bargains were struck, new acquaintanceships made, old friendships renewed, new business planned. The country seemed to enjoy such a warm sociable climate, thought Jasper for the umpteenth time, compared to the distant chilled atmosphere of the city, and he dwelt on the possibility of one day returning in his old age, then to carry on a part time practice. But he was sufficiently practical to realise that such was just an idle dream, that in this world nothing stands still, and that all these things which he now recognised as desirable would change, perhaps out of all recognition; people would change, probably even he himself. For the present, away up the centre of the wide street, the native bushes bloomed profusely, and disseminated their fragrances with abandon amid the odours of livestock, exhausts, dust and human exertion. The school children emerged as the day wore on, a noisy boisterous, sunburned, lusty crew, but courteous and respectful as the occasion demanded. The afternoon waned and the sunshine with it. The lengthening shadows reminded him of the time approaching when he must face the return journey, and he proceeded to the railhead, replete with memories of the sights and sounds of country life which must sustain him for a month until his next visit, an injection of freedom from bondage.

A couple of days elapsed and back in Mary Sutton's backyard, the sun was also warm, with little movement of air, for it was sheltered from the coastal breezes by the houses and the rise and fall of the suburban contours; it was not without humidity, and Mary lay between the grapevines bursting into leaf above her, in gorgeous relaxation. It was 4 p.m. on the Saturday following our visit to Merredin with Jasper, but she was alone. She expected David in soon. She imagined the sequence of events to come – the hum of a motor in the drive, switched suddenly to silence, heavy footsteps on the wooden front verandah, then – before she could exhaust that train of thought, she heard a person proceeding around the side of the house, and suddenly she saw him standing before her. She sat up.

'Mum,' he said.

'Hello, son,' she answered. 'I didn't hear you come up. How did you get here?'

'Friend of mine gave me a lift,' he said. 'Married chap. He lives just a couple of streets away.'

'Oh! I'm glad you've got a friend. How did the job turn out?'

'Champion! Got paid today.' He patted his hip pocket.

'Oh! That's good; and did you go to the Court?'

'Yes. Lost my licence. Only for a month though. I'll be getting it back this time four weeks.'

'Oh! son. You shouldn't have lost your licence for that, a first offence. Did you get Jasper French to speak for you?'

'No, Mum. He was in the Court and came up first off. I was going to get him, but he seemed to be in enough trouble already!'

The Judge

'Twas plain he'd aspire to the bench,
Though his practice to quit was a wrench;
And a litigious maze
For the rest of his days
Would his thirst for experience quench.

The intricacies of tort
And contract with problems were fraught;
It was quite a relief.
And indeed, past belief
When they settled them out of court.

In the matter of Porpoise v Whale,
The Defendant sought refuge in gaol;
The wily old Porpoise sought Habeas Corpus -
He was doubtful what that would entail.

In resolving a marriage pact
He showed remarkable tact;
The female de facto
Was virgo intacto
She said; but was it a fact?

Your honour, I humbly submit
If your honour deigns longer to sit
I suppress all effulgence
And crave your indulgence
But the maximum scarcely seems fit

What's important to understand is
Living was his priority, and is.
He preferred play, I guess,
But nevertheless
He laboured mutatis mutandis.

A Case Of Legal Dentrifice

The revellers scarcely noticed when he took his leave from the Club. The talk had heated up as it frequently did when he was in their midst. He had a particular quality of introducing into the conversation some controversial subject or other, however trivial, and setting one camp against another to debate it. If the interest waned he would inject fuel, by way of an inflammatory remark or pointed repartee, to give it fresh impetus, and when the argument intensified he would, as often as not, slip quietly away. He never took sides, but neither was he just a spectator, though he liked the spectacle. He enjoyed watching the behaviour of the contestants as they strove, each to outdo the other, by reason, ingenuity, gesticulation, expression, quip and every device of which they were capable, and he sought to ensure, by subtle goading, an appropriate level of vehemence and emotion. Having achieved his end, he made himself scarce. When, some time later, the drinkers looked round to him to confirm, deny, approve or censure some conclusion, he was missing. Like as not, this would make them all, on both sides, feel slightly sheepish, and at the least, somewhat abashed. It happened repeatedly, often with the same participants, and it never seemed to occur to them that it was all part of a monstrous plot carried out for that very purpose. But this serves only to illustrate that he was an observer, a student of human nature, and otherwise need not concern us in what follows.

He walked to the door of the bar, and passed through the lobby at the rear of the building, and into the open air. Apart from the throng at the bar, the precincts were quiet, and no one was in sight as he went through the parking area to his car. A dozen or so vehicles stood expectant under the stars awaiting their owners, some of whom were still at the boats, or out on the river, some at the bar, and, indeed, one had gone home by taxi, having had his 'quota' and anxious to avoid a breath test from a roving traffic patrol. The night was dark, but the stars were bright and Denis could see them reflected in the broad mass of silent water that lay like a black mirror between the beach and the opposite shore. It was about 8 p.m. on a balmy November evening. A ferry was upriver passing in the direction of Perth with a chugging noise at a distance of some five hundred metres. Its lights looked gay and festive and there was a faint sound of music emanating from the decks. In a few minutes there would be the lapping on the beach of the waves from the wake, and then afterwards all would be quiet again. Denis was pleasantly exhilarated by the sights which confronted him, no less than by the refreshment he had consumed with his companions. He reached into his pocket for the keys of his car. Muriel would be waiting for him at home, with her usual banter about being late for tea. He would be prepared for her feminine assault.

Denis Moore was a dentist, but he had been in practice for so long that the years of his industry had become a dream, sometimes pleasant, sometimes not, but merged into one long drifting sea of faces and experience, so that he could now no longer recall any specific patient or incident with clarity or accuracy, and now he stood on the brink of retirement. He still visited his surgery daily, in an aimless fashion, conscious of his limitations, ever ready to refer the difficult cases to the specialists, but mainly in response to the requests of friends and relations, with some of whom he had been dealing for decades, perhaps, maintaining his new limited clientele by reduced costs and lowered charges, but also nevertheless with a shrewd appreciation borne of long experience of the practicality of the useful expedient. He could afford to enjoy life now, and about time too. Soon he would be getting out, and a kindly nature, a wealth of experience, a tolerant humour, a pleasant personality, and considerable acumen would be forever lost to the profession. These musings occupied his thoughts as he unlocked the car, sat at the wheel and inserted the ignition key.

At the house, a mile into the suburb, Muriel sat on a sofa facing a television set. She had switched it off since the news had ended, and was occupied with crochet. It was a jacket for her new granddaughter. Muriel was a widow, and had lived alone in a flat. Denis' wife had died years ago and his family were all adult. He adored his children, but they were long since married, and he, too, had been relegated to a single existence. Muriel, likewise a victim of fickle fate, had been patient, friend, and now a fellow traveller on the ocean of inconsequence. There was a natural affinity between them, born of association, understanding, tolerance and pity. She began by coming to cook a meal for Denis from time to time, then more frequently, then she stayed a night, sometimes two nights, cleaned the house, rearranged the furniture. Finally she came to stay. As some acute observer remarked, 'I think it's permanent now – she's turned off her fridge.' They were both a trifle over seventy. Muriel was a motherly lady. She was tall and buxom, and towered over Denis who was short and stout. She was a splendid cook, after the wheat belt style, for she hailed from that district, and was of inestimable use to Denis in decorating his surgery, making curtains and managing his household and his office, and her presence in his home was as natural and as necessary as if they were man and wife. In turn he provided her with a protegé and was her purpose in life. It was with tolerant annoyance that she scolded his male shortcomings, and with contemptuous amusement that she regarded his bachelor's habits. To her he was at once lodger, child, companion and responsibility, and she was his cook, secretary, manager, housekeeper, mother, keeper, guardian.

The area in which she sat consisted of a sizeable lounge, comfortably furnished, not large, but containing sufficient amenities for the occupants: lounge suite, occasional tables, bookshelves well filled, record player, television, china cabinet – the average contents of a modern middle class suburban home in a good suburb, gently refined by an aura of professional influence. A passage led away to the front of her to the bedrooms and facilities. On her right was the front door of the house, on her left, a door leading to the back garden. At her rear was the kitchen partly screened by cupboards and supports entwined by indoor plants, and next to it, with appropriate access to each, the dining area. After the manner of wheat belt denizens of her generation, she needed no entertainment other than her crochet and her thoughts, and neither television nor radio was switched on. Having regard to her age, her circumstances and her arthritis, she was a mildly contented woman. She had security, comfort, and Denis. What more, indeed, could a woman want? It could not last, of course. Nothing does. One day the axe would fall; sickness, accident, disruption, death, destruction – sometimes the state of contentment is brought to an end by the mildest of phenomena, gently, by the entry upon the stage of a third party, or anything at all which upsets the balance of a peaceful existence. She was a philosophical woman, not given to dwelling on thoughts of the disruptive sort. She was at that moment more absorbed by thoughts of the joint she had roasted for their Saturday night repast, a substantial portion of which, complete with vegetables and gravy, reposed in the oven to keep it warm and was gradually drying to a crisp. She glanced at the clock, and squinted with annoyance. The light from the standard lamp was reflecting from the glass face, obscuring the hands. Was it 8 p.m.? While she was trying to decide, there came the sound of a motor in the drive. The noise approached to a position compatible with the carport, and stopped. A few moments later came the scraping of shoes on the mat and the back door swung open. Denis, red-faced, wild-eyed, dishevelled, slid inside, clutched the handle and closed the door behind him.

Then he turned to face his irate partner.

When there was an opinion to express, Muriel was not slow to give her version. A mild indignation at Denis' absence from dinner, forcing her to eat alone, had ripened to a healthy resentment. She had unwillingly joined the ranks of bereaved housewives languishing whilst their mates preferred the companionship of the hostelry and the solace of alcohol. The dinner had been spoiled, her work went unappreciated, the evening was gone.

'I told you dinner would be ready by half six.' The voice was strident, and the sound rang like a clarion in the silence of the room. She was about to say more, but Denis put up his hand in protest.

'Hush, Muriel, I'm in trouble, big trouble.' He spoke in a strained tone, vainly trying to maintain calm in the situation whilst restraining the volubility of his censor. There was something in his manner which achieved the latter, partly, at least.

'What is it, Denis? You've had an accident? Are you all right?' Muriel's sense of humanity took over as she looked at the comical little man and realised that all was not quite well. 'Sit down, and tell me about it.' She could discern no evidence of actual injury, but his manner was eloquent of a catastrophe of more than usual proportions. He would not sit down. While his eyes searched her face for some sign of understanding and sympathy, he stammered forth a tale of his progress from the club.

'You see, Muriel, I was driving up Stannard Street, and when I reached the top, you know there's a bend to the left. Suddenly, I saw this parked car. I didn't have a chance. It was unlit, anyway. I didn't have a chance.'

'Oh! My gosh – on your side? You hit it? Did anyone see you?'

'I went straight into the back of it. Goodness knows what damage there was. Well, I looked around and there was nobody about. I just backed off and then came straight home.'

'You look terrible. I know what's best.' Muriel marched purposefully to the dining room sideboard, stooped, and removed a bottle of brandy. She poured a generous glass and set it before him. 'Why didn't you get a taxi if you weren't able to drive?'

''Struth, Muriel, it never occurred to me. What d'you mean – able to drive? I never had much to drink!' Denis showed a little spirit through his agitation. It was all part of the permanent cut, thrust and parry with Muriel which contributed to the secret of their mutual affinity.

'Well, you were an hour over your time to get back home, and your dinner's fried to a crisp.' Muriel couldn't forbear this timely shot. 'Are you going to have it?'

'Not now, Muriel, I couldn't face it.' Normally Denis enjoyed his food. 'I think I might just have this and take it off to bed.' He picked up the glass of brandy and commenced to sip. Then he moved towards the passage. 'Cor!' He finished the brandy and walked back, placing the glass on the table. 'Think I'll have another one too.' Muriel poured more brandy into the glass.

'How's the car?' Muriel started to think of the possibility of having to walk home with the shopping.

'I haven't looked at it,' he said. 'It's in the carport. I reckoned the sooner I got home the better. The police –' He stopped at the enormity of his thoughts.

''ll get you for DD,' finished Muriel unhelpfully. She, too, was appalled by the suggestion. 'You'd better get to bed, quick. I'll tidy up here.'

'I'm all in!' Denis drained his glass and made for the bedrooms.

Muriel watched him go and turned to clear up the kitchen. The brandy bottle, uncorked, with the glass, was left standing on the coffee table. Muriel soliloquized as she worked. 'By golly, I knew it would happen some day – I've told him and told him, but he never listens to a thing I say – he's too old to be out at nights drinking beer with the young fellows. Seventy-one, and he thinks he's seventeen – he's got it all round the wrong way – wonder what the damage is – gosh, I hope I can use the car on Monday – all that shopping! – no use looking at it now, too dark out there – see it in the morning, I suppose.'

No sooner had she finished thus informing herself, when there came a knock at the front door. A startled look appeared on her face, to be replaced by one of assumed self-composure. She braced herself with some determination, made two or three perfunctory adjustments to her hair, left the kitchen and proceeded to the door from which the sound had come and opened it. Two figures stood in attitudes of waiting, heads lowered, hands hanging loosely, one a police Sergeant, closest to the door, the second a Constable, slightly to the rear, more in shadow, but nevertheless noticeably younger than his superior. The Sergeant looked up sharply on the opening of the door.

'Oh – er, Sergeant Darreby, ma'am, this is Constable Ford. There has been an accident. We are just making routine enquiries. Is that your car in the carport, ma'am?'

Muriel showed no hesitation. 'No it's not mine. It's Mr Moore's. This is his house.'

'Er, yes. Is Mr Moore at home?'

'Yes, he is. But he's gone to bed.'

'Gone to bed. Early, eh? We noted damage to the front of his car. May we have a word with him?'

'I – yes, I think so; please come in.'

'Thank you.' The two officers stepped within and looked around. 'If you will take a seat, I will rouse him.' Muriel saw them both comfortably seated and proceeded up the passage.

The Sergeant was a big man by ordinary standards, tall, broad, deep-chested, with a face that went along with it. He was of the old school, experienced, tolerant of the foibles of his fellows, aware of their faults. He was in his fifties, and had acquainted himself with the methods of the force to a degree not less than perfection. It was not easy to find fault with the running of his station when he was in charge, for he had never made a mistake in his assessment of the character of his subject. This happy knack of sizing up the other person occasionally resulted in some slight advantage accruing to him personally, and he kept his ears and eyes open just in case. In a very few minutes, Muriel emerged from the passage followed by Denis, both in carpet slippers.

Denis was otherwise fully dressed. He had removed his coat and tie to lie down, but replaced them when he heard of the police visit in the full expectation of being asked to accompany them to the station. He stood now beside Muriel, with red face and lugubrious expression, part consternation, part resignation, part bravado all showing through wide eyes. He was shorter than Muriel by all of six inches, and he looked up at her for support and introduction. He was like a small boy caught out in mischief. They were a comical couple. Looking at them, the Sergeant could not but feel a sense of real entertainment.

'This is Mr Moore,' announced Muriel.

'Good evening.' The Sergeant rose to his feet. He was a kindly man. The Constable followed suit, somewhat reluctantly, after showing surprise at his superior's deference. He already regarded Denis as a suspect to whom such consideration should not be shown. 'I am sorry to disturb you, Mr Moore, but we are making enquiries concerning an accident, and would be obliged if you would give us some assistance. Will you sit down?'

Denis sat on the edge of his chair. Muriel also took up a position from which she could maintain close contact with all that was going on. The Constable assumed a similar stand. Only the Sergeant relaxed. He resumed and occupied the full depth of his seat, leaning back with one knee crossed over the other. He believed in comfort. He took a notebook from his pocket and a pencil. 'Mr Moore, Mrs Moore has informed me that you own the Mazda sedan in the carport. Is that right?'

Denis glanced at Muriel, and, receiving her assurance, nodded to the speaker and spoke indistinguishable words of assent.

'May I know your full name?'

'Denis Harold Moore.'

'This address is 4A Cornfield Place, is that right?' Receiving confirmation, the Sergeant continued. 'What do you do for a living, sir?'

'Well I – I'm a dentist, Sergeant.'

'A dentist, eh? Is that so? Do you practise in this suburb?'

'Yes, Ashfield Terrace. Been there thirty-five years.'

'Well, I'm very glad to hear it, Mr Moore. Mr Moore, I should repeat that we are making enquiries concerning an accident,'

'Yes, Sergeant.'

'And I should inform you that we could not fail to observe that the front of your car has been damaged. I should further inform you that you may, if you wish, make a statement concerning the manner in which the damage occurred, or you may not, but in any event, anything you say in reply to our questions may be taken down. Do you wish to say anything, Mr Moore?'

Denis could not guess what had brought them to the house. He decided at once to make a full disclosure. 'Sergeant,' he said, 'I was driving from the Yacht Club. At the top of Stannard Street, I turned on the bend to the left and another vehicle was parked directly in front of me. I had no chance of avoiding it. I slammed on everything and hit it fair and square. I can tell you I was pretty shaken. I backed off and came on home. Muriel gave me a brandy. I felt bad and went to lie down and thought I'd better go down to the station in the morning.'

It was easy to see that the weight of this guilty story on Denis' mind had been considerable, and that it was with some relief that he had thus disburdened himself. Nevertheless, having thus thrown himself on the mercy of his interrogator, he was by no means confident that this was all he had to do, and he remained tense, waiting for the worst.

The Sergeant made notes of the information so far received. 'Yes,' he said, 'yes, thank you, Mr Moore.'

The Constable made as though to say something to the Sergeant, but the latter stopped him. Then, 'Mr Moore, you say you were proceeding from the Yacht Club. How long had you spent at the Club?'

'Well, Sergeant, I got there about 5.30, I suppose – two hours.'

'Did you have anything to drink while you were there?'

'Yes, Sergeant, I did.'

'What were you drinking?'

'Beer, Sergeant – 2.2 – Emu draught.'

'What were you drinking from?'

'Glasses.'

'And how many glasses would you have had when you left the Club?'

'I believe I had had five.'

'Have you had anything else?'

'No, Sergeant – er, yes, I have – Muriel gave me a glass of brandy when I came in. I was all in.'

'Two tots, you had, Denis. You asked for another and I poured it for you after the first.' This came from Muriel who had been watching events closely.

'Er, yes, well – I did that.' Denis was not quite sure that it was to his advantage to add this final indiscretion.

'Yes, thank you. That will be all, Mr Moore. I must warn you that there may be charges arising out of this incident. However, I cannot see that it will be necessary for you to come to the station with us. I do not intend to place you under arrest. You have been very frank with us. I would expect that you will hear from us within the next two weeks. Er – by the way, what is the address of your practice – Ashfield Terrace, I think you said?'

'Yes, Sergeant, No. 41.'

'Thank you, and you are normally there in working hours?'

'Ten till four, nowadays. I'm in the process of winding down.'

'I see, I see, so if I want to see you at your rooms, I'd better ring in advance.'

'Well, yes, that's so, I'd be much obliged.'

'Well, we'll make our way. I'm sorry to have troubled you. All in the course of work.' The Sergeant rose and looked at the two before him, who also came to their feet, Denis looking decidedly startled, Muriel in full control. 'Goodnight, Mr Moore. Goodnight, Mrs Moore.'

'Goodnight, Sergeant,' and the Sergeant proceeded through the front door which was opened by Muriel, followed by a slightly mystified and reluctant Constable, who had not had the opportunity to say anything, but, who had nevertheless shown obvious signs of wanting to take part. Muriel closed the door. She was blunt. 'Well that'll give them something to get their teeth into.'

''Struth, Muriel, what do you make of it?' Denis was floundering. He had never had a brush with the law in his life and was completely at sea.

'Well, I don't know. It's my bet that you won't go for DD.'

'How do you make that out?'

'They didn't give you any tests. No breathalyser or anything. The Constable had one there, but the Sergeant wouldn't hear of anything from him. It would have shown a reading anyway, because of the brandy, but that was since the accident.'

'By golly, Muriel, you're a good one. Is that why you got the bottle out in such a hurry? Usually I never see a drop of the stuff 'cause you've got it hidden in some flamin' cupboard.'

'That's –' Muriel paused to give impact to her words, 'for an emergency!'

'By the Lord, this was one o' them all right! Say, what do you think will happen?'

'You'll probably go for negligent driving, or dangerous driving, that's what, and serve you right if you do, frightening the life out of everyone like this!' By 'everyone', Muriel clearly meant herself, though she wouldn't admit for a moment that she had had a fright, or that it concerned her in the least bit. Her utterance was as much an expression of relief as anything, however, and for her, at least, the worst seemed to be over now. Denis faced a future of uncertainty.

He had read every day, in newspapers, the penalties inflicted for traffic offences, notably for driving under the influence of alcohol. He was not an adventurous driver, and did not customarily stray far off from the roads he knew, Ashfield Terrace, Cornfield Place, Pines Avenue, Riverway, which gave him access to his home, his surgery and the Yacht Club. Muriel took the car for shopping excursions, but little else. He had seen dire consequences reported in the newspapers of too cavalier uses of motor cars, occasionally to some one or other of his patients or associates at the Club. Never had any happened, nor did he think for a moment that any ever would happen to him. This was now a considerable shock, for which he had been totally unprepared. He had been comfortably going on in a little world outside all the troubles and tribulations of that other world where other people lived. Somehow or other, he had seemed to be shielded from it. Now he knew he was not. He was catapulted into it. At his age it was monstrous, it was unbelievable. He could not believe that he was the same person who had comfortably and confidently inserted his key into the ignition under the stars in the car park at the Club that evening. Clearly, things do not go on for ever. He was seventy-one now, and he supposed things must just end sometime. That sometime might be now.

When the Sergeant left Cornfield Place, he was turning over in his mind the possibilities arising out of the evening's events. He had interviewed the owner of the vehicle left standing at the kerb on the bend at the top of Stannard Street. He had been unable confidently to give any appraisal to that person of the circumstances precipitating the damage. Even now, having examined the author of the collision, he was none too sure of the success of a prosecution. The vehicle was carelessly parked, there was no doubt. It was immediately around a left bend on which there was a curtain of shrubbery, and vision would have been negative until it quite suddenly came into view. It had no lights burning, was of a dull colour, and had not made use of street lighting. The Sergeant had been involved before in a similar set of circumstances, and a lawyer had convinced a magistrate hearing them that the vehicle was a traffic hazard, and had his case dismissed. The best hopes he had or might have had were that Denis could be proved under the influence of alcohol, or that he had failed to report the accident. The first hope was blown by the brandy which Denis had clearly been at since he had come home. The second, well, Denis had told him he had intended to report it in the morning. In the circumstances this was highly credible. He was obviously very upset, and on confrontation had made a clean breast of it. Furthermore, no one had suffered any injuries. There was one more important consideration which occupied the Sergeant's mind, for he was not the man to neglect an opportunity when it knocked. Sergeant Darreby had a need of some urgent dental repairs. The condition had been getting worse over a couple of months, an upper right molar which had been filled a good many years before, and was now breaking down. The Sergeant was of a thrifty nature, not mean, but as apprehensive of the cost of dental treatment as the layman is of the receipt of a summons to attend the traffic court. For a week after his visit to Cornfield Place he debated his position. There was little to recommend a prosecution. An aptly worded report would satisfy the Inspector. By all moral standards, the little dentist had been punished enough already. His assumed bravado and absence of knowledge were enough to convince Sergeant Darreby of that: and the man was a dentist; the Sergeant wondered.

Two weeks passed, and Denis Moore's apprehension grew by the day in the face of all Muriel's attempts to calm his fears, for her efforts to do so were nullified anyway by her habit perennially of holding up his follies to ridicule. It was a situation with which he was quite unfamiliar. He had never before in his life been threatened so. He had been used in the past to stand by and see others threatened, while he advised, treated and relieved them. But now the boot was on the other foot. He grew peevish and nervous, and lay awake at nights. It was all very well, he reasoned, for Muriel. It had been all very well for him, when he was handing out advice. He knew what he was doing, and nothing could happen to him anyway. Well, now he was on the receiving end and nothing could happen to Muriel. He was not so sure that she knew what she was saying when she told him everything was going to be all right, and he was not to worry. He was worrying, and he dismissed from his mind ideas of retirement in the near future, because he feared he might need the income if he needed a lawyer, was fined, and lost his licence, or all three. Fear of the unknown possessed him. He was a babe in the woods of legal phantasmagoria. Muriel knew nothing more than he did, but she 'knew' everything would be all right, because, as she said 'she had a feeling'. The days passed slowly, one week, a fortnight; Denis knew that the machinery of the law, like the mills of God, grinds slowly, and the inaction of this period did nothing to convince him otherwise than that the day would come when he would be hauled up before the beak, just as the Sergeant had said, and then he would be dealt with as he deserved.

Such was the position on the Monday of the third week, when scarce had he opened his surgery at 10 a.m. than the telephone shook him from a reverie. Muriel was delayed in household tasks, and his first appointment had not arrived. It was a woman's voice asking for an appointment for a Mr Darreby.

Denis looked at his surgery book. The day was anything but a busy one. There were only two engagements which were likely to be protracted. Was the gentleman's case, in her opinion, an urgent one? Yes, indeed, the gentleman desired to have the matter dealt with as soon a possible, was the reply. It would be appreciated if the dentist could see him today. Then, would noon suit him? he asked. 'Admirably,' was the satisfied reply. 'Then, noon it is,' he said, and hung up the receiver. At that moment, both his first patient and Muriel, red-faced and bustling, arrived. The patient departed after a five minute examination, and when they were alone, Muriel asked:

'Who was that on the phone?'

'Oh, a new patient. A Mr Darreby. Would you write his name in the book for noon?'

'Darreby – Darreby,' Muriel's interest was aroused immediately. 'Well, you know who that is, don't you?'

'No, Muriel, no, never heard of him.'

'Never heard of him – never heard of him, of course you've heard of him. That's the police Sergeant, you mutt!' Muriel was scandalised.

'The police Sergeant! Oh-h, golly, golly, golly.' Denis was bereft of his power of speech. But he regained some of his reason. 'Well, I've accepted him as a patient, Muriel, so that's that.' It was the naked truth.

'Patient! My eye!' Muriel was scathing. 'He's not coming here as a patient! He's coming to give you a summons to court, make no mistake.'

'But the lady said his case was – urgent.' Denis was flabbergasted. 'I naturally assumed that he was in need of professional attention – er, treatment.'

'Denis,' Muriel assumed a patronising attitude, 'dear Denis, the only reason that man has for seeing you, particularly now, is to hand you a summons to court. Can't you see that?'

'Ye – es.' Denis resigned himself. 'Yes, I suppose you're right. Well, then, Muriel, this is it then.'

'This is it, right enough, you mark my words. Now is the time for you to face the music.'

It was a little harsh of Muriel to speak thus with such self-righteous authority. After all, neither Denis nor she was aware that police Sergeants rarely take upon themselves the menial task of serving process, and really Denis already had enough on his plate. Now that the axe was about to fall, it was fitting that he should be the recipient of a little sympathy. Muriel seemed to be carrying the censure bit a little far. But he was among the silent sufferers of humanity. There was no answer to Muriel's cut and dried philosophy, and he fell silently to contemplating his impending doom. Within the next hour he had one particular case of treatment requiring the benefit of his skill and experience, and he disposed of it absently, his mind half on the clock waiting for the hour of noon, but none the less efficiently, as his professional standing demanded, and the patient departed well satisfied, as so many had before him. Shortly the door of the waiting room opened, and a man entered and came to the desk. Muriel, from her place behind it, regarded him with a fixed expression. It was Sergeant Darreby right enough. He was in civilian clothes. Denis was in the surgery.

'Mr Darreby, isn't it?' lisped Muriel. 'You wish to see Mr Moore.' She was a little uncertain of herself to see him in civilian clothes, but she refused to give herself any illusions as to the reason for his visit.

'Yes, if you please, Mrs Moore. My wife made an appointment with him this morning.'

'Your wife, was it? Oh.' Muriel was mystified more, but she said, 'I'll just get him.'

Denis had already come to the door of his surgery, having guessed, if not actually heard, the nature of the proceedings. Now he was behind the desk with Muriel, looking expectantly and sheepishly up at the visitor. 'Yes, Sergeant?' he said inquiringly.

The Sergeant was uncertain how to take this approach. But he felt the situation rather better than Denis did, possibly because of the discomfort in his upper jaw.

'My name is Darreby, Sir,' he said, 'I have an appointment for 12.00 noon. Are you able to see me now?'

'But – but – but – I thought –' stammered Denis, and he looked questioningly at Muriel. She had persuaded him that he was to encounter the law.

'You thought,' pursued the Sergeant, 'that I had to follow up that little matter of the accident?'

'Well, yes,' muttered Denis, 'are – aren't you?'

'No,' said the Sergeant, 'that is all behind us. I've decided not to take any action on that.'

'You – you've decided?'

'Yes, indeed. I've decided.'

Denis was non-plussed. He was incredulous. He was elated, in that order. He glanced at Muriel in triumph. He looked at his patient.

'Step this way, Mr Darreby,' he said, in his best professional manner.

The Sergeant complied with as much alacrity as might be expected of a man with a raging toothache. An examination revealed his problem was not one which could be dealt with in a single visit, but when Denis had fairly relieved him of his immediate stress, he was feeling the benefit of vastly relieved physical symptoms. However, realising that the treatment would necessitate further, perhaps two, appointments, the spectacle of expense had begun to haunt the corridors of his imagination.

'That will be it for today, then,' Denis was saying as the Sergeant rose from the chair. 'But you'll have to see the lady at the desk for another time that suits you.'

'Thank you,' replied the Sergeant, as Denis ushered him out. 'Incidentally, do you mind if I pay for this as I go along, if you know what I mean? Can you give me an account for treatment up to this stage? I just like to know where I stand, you know.'

They were approaching the desk where Muriel had been engaged in entirely trivial, though necessary pursuits. It was lunch time, and the waiting room was empty. Muriel caught the drift of the Sergeant's enquiry and looked at Denis for direction. He had already decided. He looked at the Sergeant in triumph. He took up the appointment book which lay open on the desk, and studied it. Muriel had not written down the patient's name. He gave the Sergeant a knowing look.

'Well, Mr Darreby,' he said, 'There's no record here of your attendance. What do you say we leave it at that?'

The Sergeant's eyes twinkled. He nodded assent.

Lines Written Over One Of Those Blasted Places

I'm leaving dear old England where I haven't been for years,
And on the table near me stand some beer can souvenirs.
Are they full? They're not. They're empty. I remember now partaking
Of the contents to alleviate the pain, and stop the aching.
But the cure was not effective and, in fact, it's made it worsen –
And I sit and wallow in it and in frequent silent cursin'.
And while the other passengers are up the plane's compartment cluttering,
And I indulge myself in drink and dark nostalgic muttering,
I wonder what the next stop is, and what my stay will offer –
I don't expect much more than fresh depletions to my coffer.
For there's nothing I could find in Zurich, Delhi, Singapura
That could compare with Angleterre, of that there's nothing surer.
I've come away from relatives, and friendships I've cemented –
I dunno why I left the place, I must have been demented.
For though I've made Australia my home for many summers,
I know I got a better welcoming than other comers.
I never thought that there was any place except Australia,
And now I realise that my assessment was a failure.
If ever for the place where I was born I had affection,
It's been increased a thousandfold, that goes without reflection.
It's back to work tomorrow, when I step from this sardine can,
And while I don't believe that you could say that I'm a mean man,
To contemplate the prospect's really ghastly for the liver.
And the question looms before me – shall I end it in the river?
But when this Qantas fish tin comes to rest upon the tarmac,

And I hear shouts of 'Here she is,' 'All out,' and 'Goin' far, Mac?'
I'll very likely after all think drowning's really silly,
And I'll get home and sit myself right down and boil the billy.
I haven't got an allergy for beverages aquus,
But preferential treatment goes to beverages Bacchus.
And so besides the tea, I'll try some rather stronger fluid,
As self indulgent people everywhere, including you, would.

My Most Memorable Christmas

No it wasn't my best ever Christmas ...

Helen was in England. Our boys, four and three, were strangers to her parents.

I must say I had to fake enthusiasm about her going. A sizzler was expected here. No one knew our intentions, and I hadn't canvassed any hospitality. It was something of a last minute decision. I was too busy to go; it would have been a business no-no to absent myself even for a few days. Then there were the house and garden. Plenty to do at home. The asbestos fence was leaning crazily. But I had a dozen cold ones, and good things to eat. On the Day, I watched Mr McGraw, and generally pottered about, dodging the heat. After spending half Boxing Day straightening up the fence, I had one with the flies, went to bed, and that was that. Maybe there's something about being alone.

A week later, I got a letter.

'Darling,' I read, 'if you aren't the most wonderful husband ... fabulous trip, ... you could so little afford ... holly, turkey, plum pudding, brandy, ... Dad so pleased with the Valencia Port set up bar in corner, ... put on barman's apron. Mum ... ecstatic over koala fur handbag, ... both spoiled children rotten ... children loved their presents. Brother Mark came smoking one of those enormous cigars you sent ... beautiful aroma filled the house. Snow.

No telephone here, ... couldn't get out to ring, ... sat around gas fire, ... so much to talk about after five years ... cutting visit short. ... been here and done it now. ... all I want now ... get back to dear you. Hope you haven't had too wretched a time, ... make it up to you a thousand times ... get home. Your very own ...'

... but it was easily the most memorable!

Nuytsia Floribunda

At Christmas time in a pleasant land
        on the southern side of the oceans
Nature behaves quite contrariwise
        to your north hemispherical notions;

Ere the vernal calendar's days expire,
        like the petals that fall from a rose,
And the annual West Australian wildflower
        season draws to a close,

The countryside has a gift for everyone
        faintly concerned with festivity –
Nothing less than a timely reminder
        of glory in the nativity.

The starry November night skies
        herald a 'dawn coming up like thunder'
And the new warm days usher in
        the splendour of Nuytsia floribunda.

The West Australian Christmas tree
        flowers blossom along the coast,
For a thousand miles and into the hills,
        wherever it finds a host –

For you see – Now here's a Christmassy bit –
        if you want to be kissed, stand under –
It's really another mistletoe,
        this Nuytsia floribunda!

My Most Memorable Christmas (2)

Southampton, December, '45; the black hull of SS *Orion* loomed invitingly above the wharf. It was to be our transport, for 4,000 Australian troops actually, back home, after months, years, at war.

But so crowded; aboard, hammocks were to be slung above cleared decks on which there was just enough room for stowing personal gear immediately beneath them. Toilets – ugh!

And from date of departure, looked like we would be spending Christmas in the Red Sea!

No way!

We had friends, girl friends, rellies, whatever, back in the old Dart.

Only one thing for it – walk off: 400 of us did, anyway – typical Aussie style.

Wonder we weren't all pinched for desertion: spent overnight on the wharf: I found some clean straw: it didn't help much; it was freezing! Good thing I had my greatcoat.

Ship sailed next day without us. So much for authority. They didn't like it, of course. We were whisked off up to Nottingham and given C. B. and fatigues. Had the book thrown at us.

But we got leave for Christmas, and was it worth it? I'll say. I got a lift to London where all the action was.

The Spirit Of Christmas

The Spirit of Christmas walked abroad and he met the Man in the Street:
And he said, 'Come on over and have one at the Wayfarers' Retreat.'
The Man said, 'Too darn right I will, I feel like a drop to quaff!'
And he came out loud and clear at the job. 'Right, now I'll be knocking off!'
Upon my word, they sat and relaxed, with a tall one each in his grip,
And as for the rest of the world outside, well, they flamin' well let it rip.
They talked of the meaning of Christmas, and a good deal else as well;
Like, how best to live it up, and at the same time have a spell.
They prattled about what had happened all year, and they told some
    roguish jokes,
And as they grew better to know each other, they reckoned they're both
    good blokes.
The fella that managed the premises reckoned so too, from what he saw;
In fact, he got a bit generous himself, 'Cos that's what Christmas is for.'
The mob outside were all cheesed off, they could hear the enjoyment was rife.
And they dropped their gear as though it was hot, and they ceased from
    their toil and strife,
And in they swarmed to the Old Retreat, while the Landlord's face grew jolly.
'A Merry Christmas,' he kept on saying, 'A Merry Christmas, by Golly!'
The Spirit of Christmas slipped out almost unseen amid the throng,
On a pretext he had to see a man up the street, which wasn't wrong.
He left a little bit of himself behind in the house, you know,
Just to keep the party rolling on, and the joy from burning low.
For the Spirit of Christmas is everywhere at the season of the year
Mingled with all the sights and sounds that assail your eye and ear.
And whether you go on a razzamatazz, or stay home and mind your own
    business,
There'll always be someone who'll say, 'Good day,' and wish you a Merry
    Christmas!'

Christmas Dinner

The meeting closed late. I was already aware that I had missed my train. I had come down south by rail expecting an early finish. Now it appeared I must look for local accommodation overnight.

It was winter time, but the seaside town, so used during the summer months to the influx of holidaymakers, didn't depend for its survival on that source. I had remembered it as being something of a backwater, but it was obviously now a thriving commercial centre. It was after five and 'lighting up' had begun. Office workers, mining personnel and professionals were ceasing work or had ceased and were thronging the streets on their way home, or seeking relaxation. Rural inhabitants, dairy farmers, fruit growers, fat-lamb producers, having finished the day's business in the town, were packing up their purchases. Hotels and cafés were doing a good trade. I made my way to one of the former of which I had heard an encouraging report, and entered the bar. It was busy but not crowded. I ordered a glass of beer. On a stool beside me sat a pleasant looking man, unaccompanied. As I gave the order I felt him looking at me. Suddenly he spoke:

'Let me get it, mate. You on your own are y'? I'm only in for a couple, 'n' then I've got to push on. Have one on me.'

His approach was obviously friendly and on the basis of his averment that he was not staying long, I let him buy my drink. Perhaps he had had a good day. I took stock of him.

He was tall, broad and stooping, young, possibly 35, with a full head of dark hair combed straight back from the forehead, clear florid complexion and firm regular features. His single-breasted grey melange suit was open at the coat to display a plain white shirt and lemon yellow tie – a traveller, I reckoned him, of the commercial variety, unmistakable from his readiness to make acquaintance, to converse. I could see he was pleased with my willingness to listen to him, but I was equally sure that anyone else in the bar would have done just as well. He liked to have someone to talk to. His discourse was intelligent and punctuated with enlivening quips and phrases. I was pleasantly beguiled for half an hour while we drank our beer, and then he said, as if reluctantly, that he must be going.

'You're stopping the night then, are you? Have you booked?'
I said I hadn't booked yet but was confident of getting accommodation.
'But you're from the city, I think you said?'
'Yes, I had hoped to get back tonight.'
'Fancy going up with me? I can give you a lift.'
'I'd be very much obliged.'
'Done. I've got the jalopy out front.'

We went out, and I saw the big modern sedan. As we took our seats he asked me if I came down there often. I said I hadn't been to the town for years.

'Great place,' he said, as he started the motor. 'I've got to know it pretty well now, and we come down for holidays. Very popular. Me and the wife started spending Christmas here. The wife got fed up with getting Christmas dinner, an' all the picnic that goes on at that time of the year at home, so I suggested how about we have it at a hotel. She came up with the idea of going to the country. Well, the upshot of all that was that we came down here. Mind you, the place was already well booked, bad as the city, it was. We got berths for the night for us and the kids, and gave them their Santa Claus treatment in the morning, but do you think we could get a booking for Christmas dinner? – no way in the world, mate. Well, panic stations! "Well," I said, "we'll try elsewhere." We did, and do you know there wasn't a hope of getting a Christmas dinner in town. Wife was nearly in tears, and I could see the kids were getting the same message. Now, mate, you'll never believe this, I'll tell you what happened and God strike me dead if I'm a liar. This is gospel.'

We had left the outskirts of the little town behind us by now, and the open road allowed my driver to give the big car full opportunity to demonstrate its power. I could observe also that my companion knew every inch of the road, and I felt confident of his ability behind the wheel. He resumed his tale.

'What was I saying – oh, yes, yes. "Never mind," I said, "don't give up the ship," or something like that, "Let's get in the jalopy. We'll find somewhere, I bet." I wasn't all that confident, mind you, but it was better than sitting there looking at one another. It gave us something to do. It was getting on for midday by then, and by the time we'd paid the bill, packed up and got in the car, the hotel's guests were beginning to arrive for pre-dinner drinks. We left them to it and off. I put my foot down and we got way out in the bush. It was just trees and scrub everywhere; no sign of a town; not much sign of habitation. The road was deteriorating into a bush track. "Where are you taking us?" said my wife. The children were getting grisly, the littluns especially, and she was trying to pacify them. There were fancy biscuits and sweets in their stockings that morning, but she didn't want them to fill up on all that stuff and then not be able to eat lunch if we ever were to get some. Anyway my missus is a bit keen on her tucker too. I drove on and on. "Where are you taking us?" She was getting querulous. Trouble was I didn't have an answer to that question. I wished she'd asked me something else. I didn't know where I was going. Well, we must have been driving for a couple of hours. "I think we're lost," she said, "don't you think we'd better go back?" It was all of a quarter to two when we came to a fork in the road, and I stopped to contemplate the choice I was offered. "Which way now?" said my wife. She must have known that my guess was as good as hers, but I said confidently, as if I'd known all the time, "We'll go right," and I slipped the gear through, and put my foot down, and off we went again. I noticed as I did so that my petrol was getting low, and my throat got pretty dry all of a sudden. "We're going to have to get out and walk in a few minutes," was the thought which was uppermost in my mind. We went about a mile, and there was a left bend in the road and as I went round this, suddenly on my right I saw the loveliest sight I have ever seen before or since. I tell you, mate, Michelangelo never produced anything to come within a whisker of it. It was a canvas – if you can call it that – propped up on two posts by the roadside, about two metres long by a metre deep, and on it in great masterful strokes, brush strokes, the words "CHRISTMAS DINNER!" I nearly ran into the big karritree on my left. Even the kids stood up and cheered, and the wife put her arms around me! There was a brief opening among the trees near the sign, and through it appeared a kind of bungalow, almost indistinguishable from the bush, but definitely a house, a dwelling, and lived in. Honestly you could'a floored me with a blade of grass.

'Well, we went into this berg. On the way in I also noticed there was a bowser there. It couldn't be true. But we met the lady first. We told her we wondered if it was some kind of a mirage, hallucination, dream, whatever. She was nice. It seems her family had grown up and gone off, leaving her and her husband at home alone. He husband had told her, "What's with getting Christmas dinner now that everyone's gone?" But she had this thing about Christmas, and wanted to go ahead with it, and the result – absolute salvation for us and the young uns. There was everything, soup, turkey, ham, plum pud, the works, plus knick-knacks for the kids, an' then a glass of port while the small fry went out and explored the surrounds. Outside, the couple had kangaroos and emus in pens, and the kids had donkey rides while I was filling the tank.'

We had entered the metropolitan area, and were approaching my street south of the river, so I was giving him directions, as he was intent on seeing me to my door. I thanked him sincerely, both for the lift and the excellence of his narration.

'Yeah, well, if anyone had told me the story, I would have wondered, so I can't expect you to swallow it hook, line and sinker, and you'll just have to make whatever you can of it. But I can tell you, my wife has a very healthy opinion of her husband ever since.'

He stopped, and I alighted, thanked him again, and said goodnight.

A Christmassy Christmas Tale

Archie's Missus got on the warpath a couple of days before Christmas.

He'd started to take his holidays, but was just sitting round the house listless.

There's plenty to do round here,' she said. 'The trees and the hedge need lopping.

Only get yourself down the town today, and bring back my Christmas shopping.

Here's a list of the things I need, and the places I've usually got'm,

And there's the shopping bag you can take, it's got fifty quid at the bottom.'

She had to go to a job herself, she said, so she'd lend him her key.

'Oh, and don't forget to go,' she added, 'to Watson's, to pick up the turkey.'

So he sallied forth, for he knew full well, that the little woman meant business.

And he took the bag with the fifty quid, and the list of the things for Christmas.

He got mince pies at the pastry cook's, and nuts from the delicatessen.

From the prices he paid, he reckoned that he could show Mrs Arch a lesson.

He got the rest of the things on the list, then to Watson's to pick up the turkey,

And on his way out he ran slap bang into his old mates, Clarrie and Burkie.

They complained of a terrible thirst, and said it was something to do with season,

And reckoned he should have a drink with them, unless he had a good reason.

Burkie has got the gift of the gab, and Clarrie's a pretty fast talker,

And the new barmaid at the P & O, they said, was a little corker.

He must be a good bloke, they said, to be doing his Missus's Christmas shopping.

Their wives wouldn't let them do it, they said, and they flattered him without stopping.

So he overcame his misgivings about being loaded with Christmas turkey,

And into the P & O they stepped, Archie and Clarrie and Burkie.

It was just one round at first, of course, but then they stayed a bit longer,
And as the evening followed the day, they tried something rather stronger.
They toasted the barmaid, and sang the song – 'I wish I was single again
For when I was single, my pockets did jingle, and I wish I was single again.'
Now for most of the night at Archie's home, of discordance there were sounds
  of.
He slept with the cat in the cheerless kitchen, his little wife gave him the
  rounds of.
In the early morn, a knock at the door, and he woke from an uneasy
  slumber –
A host of suspicions, fearing the worst crowded his mind without number.
But when he opened and faced the day, lo! there stood a pretty figure
In spite of himself, as he goggled at her, his eyes grew bigger and bigger!
'Twas the barmaid from the P & O. She said, 'You were with Clarrie and
  Burkie
In the bar last night, and you left this behind, so I've brought you your
  Christmas turkey.'

Three Blind Mice [a skit]

CAST:

Mr Mouse	head of the family
Mrs Mouse	his authoritative spouse
Mike }	
Nike }	their three sons
Tike }	
The Farmer	
The Farmer's wife	

Scene I

The Mouse Family sits around a table in a rough kitchen, Mr Mouse at the head in a captain's chair, the three Mouse children in smaller chairs, facing the audience, waiting for the third course of their meal. One is reading to himself from a pamphlet, which he holds in his hands. Mrs Mouse is in the act of placing a cheesecake on the table. They make appreciative noises.

Mike: Ooh! Mum, all this and Christmas, too.

Nike: Ooh! I didn't know we were going to have dessert, as well.

Mrs Mouse: Well I just want to make sure that you all have a good meal tonight, as I'm not cooking breakfast, d'you hear? After this meal you'll have to save your appetites for Christmas dinner. Don't read at the table, Timothy.

Tike: Oh! OK (*looks up from reading*) I guess I could manage a helping of cheesecake, Mum.

Mrs Mouse: Oh! You'll manage it all right. I'm not worried about that. I'm a bit worried about you going out tonight though.

Tike: Why, Mum?

Mrs Mouse: Well, for a start, I'm afraid you'll be wasting your money

	on a lot of junk food in the shops. That's one reason why I want you all to have a good meal now. But I don't want you scurrying round the streets, either, like a lot of others I see littering up the town. I shouldn't really be letting you out at all. Timothy, are you listening? Pay attention, please. What's that you're reading?
Tike:	Er, it says here 'Report of the International Commission on the rights of the Child'.
Mrs Mouse:	Wha-a-a-t *(scandalised)* International Commission – Rights of the child! Indeed! Give it to me please. I don't know where you get these things.
Tike:	*(handing it over reluctantly)* Aw, Mum.
Mrs Mouse:	*(reading the heading)* So! This is the kind of claptrap you children learn in the city. Well, I'm not having that in my house. I've been wondering if I was right to bring you down here.
Tike:	But, Mum, we do have rights, don't we?
Mrs Mouse:	Yes you do; and the rights you have are the ones I give you, and not some fancy ideas dreamed up by a bunch of galahs in Geneva or Popocatapetl, or wherever.
Mike:	*(becoming interested)* What are our rights, Mum?
Mrs Mouse:	Never mind that now. I'm letting you go out tonight, on your own, as a special treat, and because it's Christmas Eve. You can take in the 6.30 movie, and I want you all in by half past nine. What with the way cats are these days, and the folks in the city have such a phobia about mice! So you're to go straight to the cinema, and come home right away after. Do you understand?
Nike:	Will you be – ?
Mrs Mouse:	We shall be waiting up for you, and we don't want to be worried out of our minds if you're late. Remember, we're not city folk. We only got here in the boot of the Farmer's car, and because there were biscuits in it made by the Farmer's Wife. We're country people. What d'you say, Pop? *(she sings)* Don't you agree – Parents are really at sea

	Bringing up children today.
Mr Mouse:	*(sings)* Yes, dear, I see;
	D'you think they will listen to you or me.
	Or heed what we say.
	The trouble is they don't really see
	What you mean.
Mrs Mouse:	No, they don't. They're as blind as bats. Nothing we can say is of any importance; we might as well talk to a brick wall. They think we don't live in the real world. What a farce! It's they who live in a world of their own. Really, it frightens me sometimes.
Mr Mouse:	Perhaps they would be better off here at home, spending Christmas Eve with us.
Mrs Mouse:	Oh, I've opened my mouth about it now, and I can't go back on my word, much as the prospect fills me with dread. Of course, I decided this when we were up country, and everything seemed so much safer there, didn't you think? I thought my boys could handle it, and now I'm worried. Of course it would be nice to get them off our hands for an hour or so. There are a couple of things it would be nice for us to do alone for a change.
Mr Mouse:	Such as?
Mrs Mouse:	Well, we'll go into that later. But they are big boys now, and can surely be relied on to use common sense if left to their own devices.
Mr Mouse:	It's a problem, isn't it? I can remember when I was a boy and used to ask Dad for the car, he would say, 'Ask your mother.' Then I would ask Mum, and she would say, 'Ask your father,' and so it would go on until they had a conference, and it would depend on whether I had done my jobs. Mostly I would get the car. I think I usually felt good about overcoming all the opposition in the end.
Mrs Mouse:	Looks like it's inevitable, doesn't it?
	(she sings) Well, I shall have a talk to them -
	A homily you might call it.
	We will trust you all right out alone tonight,
	So make sure you don't spoil it.

Mice children:	*(in chorus)* O, no, Mum, we won't spoil it.
Mrs Mouse:	Don't try to expect too much you know
	It's not all gold that's glistening,
	That you see in the city looking so pretty
	Now Timothy, are you listening?
Mice children:	*(in chorus)* Yes, for sure, Mum, Timothy's listening.
Mrs Mouse:	The bush and the country are streets ahead
	Of the cities and towns for wealth;
	So use your eyes, try to recognise
	The ways to preserve your health.
Mice children:	*(in chorus)* We'll always preserve our health.
Mrs Mouse:	By health I include your personal safety
	From dangers you'll find in the city,
	Like the little cheese scraps that you see in the traps
	And the swift sure paws of kitty.
Mice children:	*(in chorus)* Oh! We'll circumnavigate kitty.
Mrs Mouse:	It's as well to be always on your guard -
	We can do without sickness and sorrow;
	So be on your way, and heed what I say,
	And remember it's Christmas tomorrow.
Mice children:	*(in chorus)*We'll remember it's Christmas tomorrow.
	Exit the children.
Mrs Mouse:	I hope they don't get up to any mischief.
Mr Mouse:	Well, we've done our best, and if they do heed our warnings. And if they do go straight to the cinema, and if they do go things should work out.
Mrs Mouse:	If – if – if – if wishes were horses, beggars would ride. Well, what are the traps? – Pah – mustn't use that word. What are the hazards? They've got to pass the car, haven't they? Do you think they might fossick about there to try and find more of those biscuit crumbs? They certainly were nice you know. We should go and have another look ourselves – but there, mustn't set a bad example, must we? They'll learn enough out there without us teaching them. I'd better get on with these Christmas preparations. There's a lot to do yet. But if we get a chance we'll think about it.

Mr Mouse:	Yes, let's get on with it. I'll give you a hand. It'll help us to stop worrying about them. Anyway, what was that stuff Timothy was reading?
Mrs Mouse:	Oh! I put it in the bin. I'm not having that around, letting people think I believe in it. A lot of rubbish talked about by people who haven't the slightest idea what it's like in real life; and putting false ideas into the heads of children. I haven't any patience with it, and it just does more harm than good. We're the ones who have to bear the consequences of their interference, and the less we see of the stupid rules the better.
Mr Mouse:	I can't say that I disagree with you.
Mrs Mouse:	And what makes me mad is that they get paid for all that stuff they turn out. *(Curtain)*

End of Scene I

Scene II

The Farmer's Wife is in her kitchen. She and her husband have brought in things from the car. The Farmer is hovering around.

Farmer's Wife:	Just look at these biscuits! I was hoping to have them on the table tomorrow, for nibbles with a drink before Christmas Dinner, but the wretched mice – I took such care with them, and they turned out beautifully – look! *(as she tilts the parcel in her arms, biscuit crumbs litter the table and floor)* – chewed all through the wrapping right into them – half of them are ruined. I can't believe there were mice in the boot of the car. Did you see anything?
Farmer:	Not a whisker. Can't understand how mice can have got into the boot. There must be a gap in the bodywork some-where. I'll have to see to that. Can't do anything tonight, can we? We could, I suppose. Put those down a minute and come out with me. I don't like the thought of mice running round the place. They might still be there. *(Farmer's Wife sets parcels on the table and they go out as she answers.)*
Farmer's Wife:	I'll take this carving knife, and I'll teach them to raid my Christmas goodies.

(Exit Farmer and Farmer's Wife. Enter the three Mice children, Mike, Nike and Tike.)

Mike: Here we are in the kitchen. What, no one here! I can smell biscuits. They must be here, somewhere.

Mike: On the table, I reckon.

Tike: Let's have a look. I'll get on this chair. *(climbs into a chair)* Yes. Oh, beauty. I can see them, come on now, I'll push a couple over the edge. Here! Watch out! *(biscuits fall off the table as he noses them.)*

Mike and Nike: *(they do a little dance around the fallen biscuits.)*

O! what a treat, what a treat,
It's Christmas already, it seems.
Our city visit's a great success.
Exceeding our wildest dreams.
The farmer's wife is a very good cook,
Preparing this food with such taste.
The opportunity doesn't knock often,
So let's fall to and make haste.
What super luck to happen on these
While Farmer and Wife are out.
O! Christmas time is the time for fun
Without a shadow of doubt.
We'll keep our eyes open in case they return
And our ears cocked for unusual noises
While we tuck into this delightful food –
O! but listen, do I hear voices?

Farmer: *(from without)* Yes, there's a place big enough for them to have got into the boot, all right. I'd better get something done about that, dear.

(the mice scurry into a corner, scattering crumbs as the Farmer and Farmer's Wife enter)

Farmer's Wife: Oh! Thank you. Yes that would be a help, and – oh! my goodness! Look at this! *(voice rises to a screech)* Something's been here in the little time we were out. Mice again! The whole place must be infested with mice. Where are they? They can't be far. *(brandishing the carving knife as she discovers the broken fragments on the floor)*

	I'll catch them. *(she adopts a menacing attitude)* I'll cut the tails off them! *(she rampages round the room)*
Farmer:	You'll never catch them – they probably heard us coming. *(the mice are cowering in the shadows in cold fear)*
Mike:	Oh! dear, we shouldn't have lingered, you know. *(he sings)*

A shadow has fallen across our plans,
The best laid they surely weren't.
We're into deep water right over our heads
And we've gotten our fingers burnt.
O, what shall we do? – if only we
Had Mother and Dad to consult.
They'd know what to do, though they'd probably say
It's our own darn silly fault.

Nike: Yes, yes, if I thought this would happen, I'd never never have left home. *(sings)*

How quickly the tide of fortune turns
In the life of the hapless mouse!
A moment's delight is completely destroyed
By a Farmer and irate spouse.
The Farmer's Wife will make short work of us
In her fit of exasperation.
We'd all be extinct if she had her way –
Don't they know about conservation?

Tike: Never mind about all that, now; let's watch for a chance to get out of this, or we'll never get home again.

Nike: Mind your tails, for heaven's sake. I don't like the look of that carving knife. Yes, I wish I'd stayed at home now. We must have been blind not to see it's a minefield out here.

Tike: Yes, Mum had plenty of nice things to eat anyway. That cheesecake seems better every minute, now – it is Christmas Eve too – p'raps it would have been best to go straight to that movie; p'raps after we get out of this, – if we ever do. Hey! shall we make a run for it?

(During this exchange, the Farmer's Wife is raging round the kitchen table, looking in corners, behind furniture,

	everywhere, yet all the time missing the three miscreants, and shouting the most terrifying threats)
Farmer's Wife:	I'll cut them to pieces, if I find them. There won't be a mouse within miles of this place, by the time I've finished with them. Just give me a chance to use this. *(and so on from one end of the kitchen to the other.)*
Farmer:	But darling, it's Christmas.
Farmer's Wife:	I'll get 'em, Christmas or no Christmas. Anyway, they're spoiling Christmas for me. *(here she turns back to her husband, and approaches him whilst speaking, her back to the youngsters)* How do you think I can enjoy Christmas with a lot of beastly mice eating it up before I can even taste it?
Mike:	Yes! Now! Run for the door. *(they sprint in the direction of the Farmer's Wife. The Farmer sees them, and they realise they have been seen, and fall over each other in their haste).*
Farmer:	Look, there they are, three of them. They can't see what they're doing. *(he bursts into a loud guffaw. His wife spins round but the mice elude her and escape in utter confusion through a door, and run straight into the arms of their father and mother; there is pandemonium as they disappear together into the darkness)*
Farmer:	*(sings)* Three blind mice,
	Three blind mice,
	See how they run,
	See how they run,
	They all run after the Farmer's Wife,
	She'll cut off their tails with a carving knife
	Did you ever see such a thing in your life
	As three blind mice.
Farmer's Wife:	It's all very well for you to laugh. *(Curtain)*

End of Scene II

Scene III

The scene is the Mouse children's bedroom. The three children are in a large bed, lying side by side, looking chastened. Mrs Mouse is standing beside the bed, reading the Riot Act as they say. Mr Mouse is right beside her backing her up.

Mrs Mouse:	Well, let it be a lesson to you. And if you've learned it there will be something gained from this evening's events. But remember this, the whole thing could have ended in absolute disaster, and you could have all lost your tails, 'cos that's what happens to the like of you that tangle with a farmer's wife, it's written. Just to think that there might have been a dreadful tragedy on this Christmas Eve. Why, Mummy might have been deprived of the pleasure of hanging up your Christmas stockings (not that there's much room in them) – and seeing your bright happy faces on Christmas morning – oh! it just doesn't bear thinking about. And your Dad enjoys it all quite as much, though he may not show it always. What luck we were both there! What luck, I say, to be on the spot and rescue you from a dreadful fate.
Tike:	Please, Mummy, may I ask a question?
Mrs Mouse:	Question? What question, my child? It's time for you all to go to sleep. It's Christmas tomorrow, and you'll all need all your energy. We can't be standing here all night answering questions. As far as I can see, there's nothing more to be said. What do you say, my dear? *(to Mr Mouse)*
Mr Mouse:	I think, my dear, he probably wants to say what a coincidence it was, meeting us there.
Mrs Mouse:	Is that it, child? What is your question?
Tike:	I just wanted to know, Mummy, how you came to be there.
Mrs Mouse:	How we came to be there – how we came – well, we just happened to be there, *(embarrassed)* we, er – we, er, well, we thought it would be a good idea, we wanted, in fact, to get a couple of those biscuits for your Dad and me to have a drink with before Christmas dinner tomorrow. Does that answer your question?
Mike: } Nike: } Tike: }	*(In unison)* Ooooh! *(they all look at each other)*
Mrs Mouse:	And you needn't look like that, either. *(Curtain)*

Autumn

Autumn comes round but once a year;
So does the day of your birthday, dear.
I smiled and stood there to welcome you;
It seemed that you looked me through and through.
Distant, aloof and proud and haughty –
Autumn is fancy free and naughty.
I wished you well and stroked your chin,
(Seeking approval thus to win)
I fancied your touch to be rather cold –
Autumn is warm and brown and gold.
Lavish and fickle is Autumn's glance,
Leading us people a merry dance –
Winds on the treetops and sun on the plain!
Is something you've eaten, dear, causing you pain?
Are you afraid your tale's been told?
Or is it that we're all growing old?
I've searched in my head for an adequate reason –
Perhaps, dear, it's just that you're out of season!

Profile Of A Forebear

Grandad dusted himself down and came in from the fowl pen. He was not sure whether he had collected all the eggs or not. The rooster which he had installed with the hens had never accustomed itself to his intrusion. It exhibited an intense personal antipathy to the very sight of him if he only so much as came within twenty feet of the enclosure. As to entering, if only to feed the flock, it was unrestrained. He had always to take in a stick to ward off its attacks, in spite of which the fowl scratched his hands, buffeted his legs, and would have pecked his very face, but that he did, as expeditiously as he could, what he simply had to do, and beat a hasty retreat to avoid as much unpleasantness as possible. It was a great Rhode Island Red, a magnificent specimen, weighing perhaps thirty pounds, of which he might have been justly proud, and might well have boasted about to his friends, for he liked to impress people, but his leanings in the direction of magniloquence and self aggrandisement were quite immolated by the cock's fury and disdain of him. He resented being denigrated, most of all by a rooster. There was obviously only one destiny for that bird. The seeds of an idea for a Christmas repast were well and truly sown.

The thought helped him to reassert his composure and he proceeded to the kitchen, placed the eggs on the rack, and washed his hands. It was breakfast time, and as he entered the dining room, Grandma was in the act of setting down his bacon and eggs. The family gathered.

'Have you got pepper and salt, Bet?'

'On the table, Will.'

This time honoured exchange was followed by a sequence no less traditional to the O'Reilly clan. Seated, Grandad took up the salt shaker, and for all of twenty seconds shook it vigorously over his plate, whilst the others regarded him with silent awe, and Grandma was moved to remark:

'It is not necessary to put all that salt on your food, Will, it's very bad for you to have so much salt.' But this well intentioned solicitude evoked no response audible or visible. He next took the pepper and shook it with similar abandonment, and at such an elevation that clouds wafted across the little space that encompassed his features, like the mists that drift across the face of Venus in a galactic documentary. The consequence was natural and predictable; his head and shoulders were convulsed in a catastrophic sneeze as he twisted them abruptly to his right, bringing that hand to his mouth, two, three, perhaps four times. These explosions behind him, he then commenced his meal. The others – there were three children, steps and stairs – and Grandma glanced at each other, eyebrows slightly raised. It was a replay of the action which preceded every meal.

He never seemed to appreciate that the pepper would make him sneeze.

Grandad was a small man, and his movements were deliberate and dignified. His employment was inauspicious, but he endeavoured to conduct himself in a manner and on a plane seemingly above that which his own occupation might suggest. He stood straight, and stepped gracefully as he walked. He invariably wore a dark grey three-piece tweed suit, gold watch chain arrayed across the front of the waistcoat and fob watch reposing in the vest pocket, and he was rarely without his coat. His black shoes shone so that you might imagine you could see your face in them, and he habitually wore a black Homburg, brushed and smart. He took pride in his appearance. In the city a great deal of bomb debris was being cleared and rebuilding done, and it was not uncommon to see him standing, watching the workmen at their jobs, his feet in the 'at ease' position, coat open, thumbs tucked into waistcoat armholes, looking for all the world as if he were the owner, or architect at least, and such that a workman passing by was moved to touch his cap and murmur 'Morning Guv,' and Grandad would acknowledge the salute with the slightest inclination of the head and curt response, as he might have answered with authority, 'Right, carry on.' Grandma used to watch him with mild derision. 'Look at him,' she would say. 'Look at him. He's enjoying that.'

He wore the ubiquitous grey suit and Homburg hat as though they were part of him, even to the beach, where he would hire a deck chair and set it on the sand, sit on it, barefooted, shoes and socks beside him, trousers cuffs minimally rolled, for that was his concession to the ravages of salt water, and still with his hat firmly on his head. One might imagine him on the deck of the *Titanic*, as the giant ship rocked and heaved, buffeted by polar ice, swamped by mountains of water, derelict, doomed, but Grandad in his Homburg, unperturbed, imperturbable.

He was not a jolly man, that is, during the week at home, and at work, he was not to be described as jocund. He was strangely silent, withdrawn, distant, unapproachable. Weekends effected that magic transformation from gloom to brightness, from doom to rebirth; because that was when Grandad went to the pub. No-one in his family ever became acquainted with what went on in the bar of the 'Exchange', but it was to their unfailing amazement and relief (except for Grandma who had scant sympathy with Grandad's weaknesses) when he emerged, smiling, effusive, jocose, after an hour or so in that convivial atmosphere. A little of the dignity born of remoteness was depleted, the social barrier that enveloped him at other times was somehow ruptured, and the generous spirit streamed through the fissure. He was more responsive, accessible. His older daughter, Annabelle, was wont on occasions to take advantage of these moments of affability to ask him whether he would not be so kind as to contribute a little to the expense of a frock she wanted for a dance. She was a pretty girl, she had taking ways, and her timing was precision itself, so that he unfailingly fell an easy prey.

But daughters grow up and wed, and sometimes live far away, and in ever such a few short years it seemed that this one was settled with a husband and three children – a boy and two girls – in seeming replication of her parents, at a seaside resort in faraway Australia. She arranged for Grandad and Grandma to visit her. It was in the receding days of ocean travel, and they enjoyed a shipboard holiday and a few months sojourn at Annabelle's unique little home.

Grandad enjoyed an occasional visit to the alehouse in the village. Sometimes he had the opportunity of being driven there by a friend and neighbour and fellow countryman whom we shall call Dixie, in his little car. Dixie had bad hips and walked with a stick, but he liked a drink in good company when he came home from work.

One other occupant of the little house, whose arrival had been somewhat unexpected, but nevertheless unavoidable, cannot be overlooked. Lisette was Annabelle's friend, They had been at school together. When the latter migrated to Australia, Lisette had accompanied her, and together they faced the thrills and the ordeals of settling into an adopted country. But Lisette was the less fortunate of them. She entered into an unsatisfactory liaison, and, whether by design or accident, for it was never known, or even discussed, fell pregnant. When Annabelle learned of this, there was no question but that Lisette should live out her confinement under her roof. There was no difficulty attending this arrangement to anyone but Grandad. His upbringing – shall we ascribe it to the reign of that glorious sovereign? – would not permit him to offer any sympathy with her condition, or even to recognize her presence in the house. He refrained from acknowledging, even from speaking to her. He voiced his distaste to Grandma. It is not known whether Lisette felt any embarrassment from this attitude, for she was a close one, and no-one knew what she was feeling, and in any event, she was not in a position to complain. As for Grandma, she did not share Grandad's 'holier than thou' attitude; in fact, she had scant sympathy with his foibles and, privately, she thought his attitude rather hypocritical. Again, privately, she would not have denied Lisette some appreciation of another woman's problems. But, to save face, she quietly remonstrated with Annabelle a little.

'Perhaps you shouldn't have invited us while Lisette was here like this, dear,' she would say from time to time.

Which was mechanically impracticable, of course, because the arrangements for her and Grandad to visit were already in operation when Lisette's predicament became known.

Lisette had a little room, sometimes designated the 'sewing room', downstairs. She had returned to it one evening, and was awaiting dinner being prepared by Annabelle and her mother up in the kitchen, when there came something of a clatter up the concrete ramp leading from the street to the carport past her room to the front door. Then a knock and Dixie called out.

Hearing the knock, Annabelle went to the head of the stairs and soon realised that something was amiss. She ran down and opened the door. Dixie interrupted any question forming on her lips. 'Annabelle,' he said, 'Your dad.' It was his stick which had made the clatter as he had with difficulty mounted the ramp and he was out of breath and rather self-consciously embarrassed by the news he had to break. 'Your dad has passed out. I don't think he's used to the beer, and then he would insist on having a brandy before leaving the bar.' Lisette had by this time come out of her room, apprehending an emergency, 'Can you give me a hand,' continued Dixie, 'to get him into the house?'

'Oh, Dixie, I'm sorry, yes, of course,' said Annabelle. 'Lisette, you'll give me a hand, won't you? Dixie, where is he?'

'He's in the car. I couldn't manage him.'

'No, of course not. Don't you worry.' It was true. Grandad was out cold. True, he was no heavyweight. A puff of wind might blow him away, you might say, but Annabelle knew well that for a man who relied for his mobility on a walking stick, a limp body would have been an impossible burden.

'Oh my goodness,' said Annabelle as they approached the car, 'You take his legs, will you, Lisette? And I'll take his head and arms.'

Together they lifted him from the car, carried him up the ramp and into the house, followed by Dixie, hobbling with his stick, feeling vaguely guilty. Into the hall and up the stairs past the landing they managed very well; and all the while Grandad lay in sublime unconsciousness of their tender ministrations.

But the cause of the trouble had not escaped Grandma. The enormity of Grandad's self inflicted indisposition was almost more than she could fairly bear, and she had prepared herself for what she must certainly do. All her precepts of refinement and proper conduct were deeply wounded, and she had worked herself into a perfect fury of embarrassment and distaste; with her umbrella which she had fetched immediately the truth dawned, the unpalatable truth, she was awaiting the little party at the head of the stairs.

'Let me get at him! Let me get at him!' she screamed, 'I'll kill him. I'll kill him! Showing me up like this. Humiliating me in someone else's house.'

She held the umbrella in the 'strike' position, from which best to deliver the terminal or other mutilatory blow, or blows, for it was unlikely, judging by her demeanour, that she would have been satisfied with a single blow, even a terminal one.

But for this time, while this tirade continued, Grandad lay in a swoon, blissfully unaware that his person was under threat.

In fact both girls were obliged, in carrying Grandad, to stoop partly over his inert form, and Grandma had to hold her fire somewhat, otherwise she was in danger of striking them both down, or at least one of them. Dixie also gallantly tried to ward off her attacks.

'It's all right, Mrs O'Reilly, it's all right,' he protested, hobbling on his stick, and interposing himself and it, as discreetly as he could, between Grandma and her quarry.

But Grandad remained ignorant of the brave stand made by his friend against the imminent massacre.

The girls' progress was much impeded by this storm of attack and defence, but by degrees and with some difficulty, they man-handled the limp figure to the first floor unharmed, and up the passage to his room. They laid him on the bed and closed his door and turned to face Grandma. Grandma's eyes were wide, and her face was red. One had the impression that if she had been an electric light bulb, she would have popped a filament.

'Mother,' said Annabelle as soon as she had closed the door behind Grandad, 'I think you'd better come and have a nice cup of tea.'

'I'm so ashamed,' said Grandma, 'how could he do this to me? Wait till I get him, the wretch.'

It seems she verbally took him to task from the moment he recovered consciousness.

This story must surely have a moral, and it must be 'Blessed are the meek'. In the morning, there was a chastened Grandad, and Lisette the scorned, Lisette the ostracised, the despised, the humble, the uncomplaining, received from him an apology, he having pocketed his pride, his dignity, his condescension.

It was an occasion when he was able to show that he could rise above himself.

July Downunder

Winter's damp tweedies and muddy shoes
    Never infect us with birthday blues.
How can your asteroids come to be cast
    In the middle of all this icy blast?
In twisted branches and scurrying leaves?
    Under your consecrated eaves
I arrive like an Eskimo, muffed to the chin –
    Mentally ill-equipped, yang to yin.
Off come the overcoats, jumpers and scarves –
    Here, it seems, things don't get done by halves.
Rain is the rooftop, and dullness the window
    Here in our decaffeinated limbo –
Computed nutriment, cosiness, shelter –
    Outside the leaves go helter skelter!

The Wages of Romance

When the shearers came, Sue Gilming fell in love with the rouseabout. They were only there a week. There were roughly two thousand sheep, but the two men were 'gun' shearers, and could 'knock off' a couple of hundred each per day with the blades. They had their meals at the homestead. where Sue worked helping with the household duties in general, and from the first day she couldn't keep her eyes off the boy. He was certainly a well set up lad, strong, with good shoulders and head set well back on them. He had fair tousled hair, which, however unruly, seemed always somehow to be in place. He never wore a hat. His name was Pat Clohessy and he had a face ever ready to break into a smile, didn't smoke, drink? – well, hardly ever, just worked and ate and slept and was content. He rather fancied Sue Gilming too, and in the few short days the shearing lasted, before you could fairly recite 'Click go the Shears', they were out walking together in the evenings.

The farmer, Alec McAllister, and his wife Evelyn remarked on this flurry of activity on the part of Cupid, and thought it was rather sweet. There wasn't much social life out there in the Styx for Sue, they said, and she was welcome to a little society, especially from such a nice young man. She was just a girl, and he was just a boy. There couldn't be as much as forty years in their combined ages, and both were very well balanced young people.

Every day, Pat gathered and threw the fleeces, skirted and classed, and attended to all those multifarious jobs which have given their name to the rouseabout's vocation, with, to the discerning eye, renewed interest and redoubled vigour. He was worth his two pounds per week wages, and no mistake.

The balmy autumn twilight was conducive to endless strolling in the creek bed, sitting on logs and talking of life and love, and lounging on the stack of seed wheat stored in second-hand bags under cover of the machinery shed. Thither they repaired together when the day's work was done, and the last glow of the western sky finally lost itself in the darkness which hung in mystery upon the fields. On the fifth evening of the shearers' stay, their job was finished, and Pat and Sue could only look forward to a morrow when they would be irrevocably separated, when he would be moving on from early morning to other work, new surrounds, fresh pastures.

A good day's work in the shed, or in the house, from daylight to nightfall is a natural enough soporific. As they lay together on the all accommodating stack of seed wheat, each with an arm round the other, both fell fast asleep.

They lay still, in the deep undisturbed sleep of the young. The air was motionless; not a breath of wind ruffled the stillness, nothing but the haunting cry of the mopoke broke the silence. Thus they remained unwittingly, and the night wore on; but in the early hours a rooster crew. Pat was first to stir; uneasily, at first, but with growing realisation of their circumstances. He had no watch, but guessed it was not far from dawn. He saw the morning star well above the horizon.

'Sue,' he said, 'Sue, wake up. Wake up, Sue. I've got to get back.'

She was as if drugged, but rallied at the urgency of his tone. She clung to him. 'Are you all right?' she whispered.

'Yes, Sue, I'm all right, I love you,' he said. 'Can you get home all right?' and he kissed her.

'Yes,' she said.

'I must go,' he said.

And that was the last they saw of each other.

Pat led a somewhat nomadic existence, removing constantly from one farm to another with the shearing gang. Weekends, he was sometimes in small towns with few facilities, and then for short periods only, mainly to pick up stores or equipment. There was little time or opportunity for him to keep in touch with anybody, even his parents' home, which indeed was in another state. He never forgot Sue, but in the exigencies of continual movement, of keeping his job and earning a living, the memory of their short association inevitably faded.

With Sue, circumstances differed substantially. The McAllisters appreciated her assistance, looked after her needs and liked her as a person. They would have gone to lengths beyond those normally expected of an employer for a worker to retain her services. She felt secure, appreciated and loved, and gave of herself unstintingly. Their son Angus, who was just eight, was fond of her, too, though he was blissfully unaware of and indifferent to the ways of adults, so long as he received consideration for his own needs, which, in any event, was undisputed. His mother had ambitions for him, and hoped to send him to high school when he grew a little older. She was conscious of the drudgery of farm life, and wanted better conditions for their boy. Doctors and bankers were in the social ascendency in those early days. She planned for him to become a doctor. A farmer's hands were hard and rough and scarred, but a doctor's were soft and sensitive. She herself was not discontented with her lot, but she saw it as a stepping stone for better things for her son.

Sue was a small girl, possibly five feet two inches in height, but of sturdy build, and ever active. Without suggestion of restlessness, she was continuously on the move, and her glance darted hither and thither, seeming never to miss a thing which went on around her. She had curiously small attractive features, vaguely reminiscent of a little monkey, ever anticipating, it seemed, each person's intention and train of thought.

She accepted that Pat would move on to other arenas. The memory of their association buoyed her, and she was too practical to think there was any other way of life. She did not miss him; in some way it seemed that he would always be with her. Her way of life was not disturbed; she still had her work to do, still had the friendship and support of the farmer and his wife, and when she went to bed at night, she felt as though she belonged, just as much as she ever had, and would so continue. The days wore on for so long, and there was little at first, if anything, to denote any change in her way of life, until within the space of a few weeks it became increasingly evident that her body did not feel quite the same as before. There were certain signs, changes, mildly disquieting, perhaps, but unmistakable. At first she dismissed them, but finally they became impossible to ignore, and she was not able to deny to herself that she had indeed conceived. Her mind had run the gauntlet of a variety of emotions: mystification, suspicion, disbelief, apprehension, realisation, alarm, and when the truth dawned, momentarily, sheer panic. But she was too strong a character to permit the onset of chaos or despair to descend upon her. She determined not to mention anything to anybody. They would find out of course, and what they did then was their business, and a measure of their attachment to her. Her situation was her business and hers exclusively, and she would deal with the problems that arose from it as they appeared.

It lay within the province of the McAllisters to ameliorate her problems. Within the first few months, Evelyn McAllister came to suspect that something was amiss, and then quite by accident, all was revealed. She had said nothing to Sue, and there was nothing in Sue's demeanour which gave her away, but Evelyn knew, and Sue knew that she knew, and neither said anything to the other about it. Perhaps there is mutual understanding among the female sector on these matters of a delicate nature. Evelyn confided in her husband, but cautioned him to remain silent on the subject.

'I suppose she'll want to leave us,' he commented. 'Will she be wanting to go to the father?'

Evelyn did not know, and refused to be drawn on the possibilities for Sue's future. 'It's not really our business,' she told him.

In due course, Sue managed to have an examination by a doctor in their district, and was able to fix a date when the baby might be expected. Alec McAllister was really too busy to concern himself with the intimate problems of his female employee. The seasonal farm operations were as much as he cared to be involved in. The seed wheat, so reminiscent to Sue of her romantic adventure, was taken from the shed and sown in a southerly paddock, whence developed a fine crop for harvest, and the seasonal work of the farm went on as usual. Christmas time came and went. Angus was nine now; he was becoming more conscious of the workings of the organisation of which he was so far a very minor part, and his father was grooming him in minor tasks about the property, so that he might be useful as long as he remained there. After the crops were taken off, there was something of a lull in activity on the farm. It was a period of relaxation, and Evelyn and Alec McAllister took the opportunity, from time to time, briefly to get away by themselves. Sue was quite obviously pregnant now. Evelyn was careful to see that she was spared any tiring or heavy work, though, to her credit, to do so placed additional duty on herself. Still there was no open discussion of the subject; it was as much by guess as by the sharing of confidences that she became aware of the doctor's assessment of the date the new arrival might be expected. Sue was alert and as well as ever. She appeared to be positively blooming, though she was grateful for her mistress's consideration, and dutifully prepared vegetables, stitched, set table, swept and dusted, and was practically as fully occupied as ever she had been. Alec McAllister remained aloof, as though the situation did not exist, though it would hardly be possible to ignore it when the baby appeared. That, by all accounts, was two weeks away. The business of the farm proceeded as usual. He took note of an advertisement in the *Farmer's Gazette* of a sale by a farmer in the district. It was a sell-out, by auction. He knew of the property. The advertisement stated that all machinery and stock were to be offered as well as house contents and household equipment. He was interested because a combined cultivator drill was specified, and he wanted to see if it could be had for a price he was prepared to pay. He discussed it with Evelyn, and she also evinced an interest because she would like to see the lots comprising household contents. It was eighteen miles away, and the bidding was to commence at 9 a.m. They would have to make an early start.

Angus was told to remain and spend the day in the field with the sheep. They were feeding in stubble bordering on unfenced lake country, and it was necessary to ensure that they did not stray into the low scrub. He had done likewise on several previous occasions since harvest. It was the stubble from the crop about a mile to the south of the house, approximately four hundred acres. Sue was able to look forward to a comparatively leisurely day. The McAllisters were expected home by dusk. Plans for the day were simple, conclusive and unequivocal, and master and mistress departed in the little sulky immediately after an early breakfast.

Sue's first care was cutting Angus' lunch: bread and dripping sandwiches well laced with the good brown meat juice and jelly from the roast of the previous night; cold lamb sandwiches with cauliflower pickle; a good slice of plum cake and a couple of figs; the lot encased in grapevine leaves, wrapped in two sheets of newspaper and slipped into a brown paper bag for easy portability. This she handed over, and having been abroad since before six as usual, decided she would be well advised to take a few minutes rest in her little room.

Angus set forth. He had nearly a mile to walk. Normally he might have ridden the pony, but she was being used for the sulky. It was going to be a hot day, probably touching 100 degrees Fahrenheit, and he took a waterbag. The sheep had been brought down that morning from the yards in which they had been penned overnight to protect them from dingoes, and were grazing peacefully. The dam still held water; the farm was situated on a level plain surrounded by low unobtrusive hills, on which, all around, similar farms straddled where clearing had taken place, the fence lines and timbered patches clearly outlining the fallowed and stubble paddocks. He prepared for a long day of monotony on which he could well expect that nothing would happen. A little society would have been welcome, but it was enough to feel that home was there if he needed it, and anyway, he had done all this before, and he was not perturbed. He was alone with this thoughts. To the south, he mused, five miles away, were the hills where the train climbed on its long journey east. At nights, he could lie on his bed under the homestead verandah, and watch as the lights mounted the gentle slopes, the sounds of the engine's labour only audible if the night were perfectly still. He remembered that when grasshoppers were in plague proportions, the lines became slippery with their crushed bodies, and the wheels spun so that the engine made hard work of the gradual ascent. To the east lay a chain of salt lakes, a haven for waterfowl in winter but dry in summer, and a habitat for dingoes. He recalled the eerie feeling he had always had when the sound of their howling floated up to the homestead at night, accompanied by the plaintive whistles of curlews. There were nights on which bushmen sat around their campfires, swapping ghost stories, and yarns about the stillness and the vast open space. When he went out at night in the bush, he felt the urge to sing and shout, mindful of the stories that had been told in his hearing; it seemed to take his mind off the ominous silence, and gave some sort of feeling of security.

The sheep were all out in the long stubble when he arrived, but as the day wore on and the summer's heat increased they were prone to gather in folds, hundreds at a time, in shade where possible, on the banks of the dam and elsewhere, simply at random. The lake at the foot of the paddock, after winter rains so cool and blue, was now almost dried to a pan, and had failed to attract any of the flock. Its winter population of black swans, teal, mountain duck and avocets had departed for wetter areas. The morning wore on, and as the sheep settled down in their chosen places, he moved to a shelter to have his lunch. It was no more than a roughly erected brush canopy, but it offered a few square feet of shade. He was used to exposure to the sun, from journeying to and from school, and since Christmas had been out of doors every day, sometimes all day. He was quite brown, slightly freckled, vibrantly healthy; it was February and shortly he would be resuming school. He lifted the water bag to his mouth, and suddenly, in a moment of consternation, realised that he had left his lunch at home.

He was aghast; he remembered distinctly receiving it from Sue and laying it on his verandah bed while he filled the waterbag; and now, he realised, he was ravenous. There was only one thing to do – go home for it. The sheep were quiet, and not likely to move while the heat was on. The sooner he got back with it the better. Sue would chide him, of course, but there was no help for it. He started home forthwith.

When Sue had gone to her room to lie down, 'for a few minutes', she had felt fatigued, and promptly fell fast asleep. She felt, perhaps, a trifle more cumbersome than was usual for her. She was certainly grateful for an easier day, and put herself down on the bed with considerable relief. For some hours she had only herself to think about. It was some time before she awoke. It was hot, and she realised that she needed the window open. She needed more air. It was hot air. Resuming her reclining position, she found that she needed to shed some of her clothes; then it came to her that her abdomen was in movement. She was contorting. She was seized with alarm. She was having contractions. The baby was coming. She got up; then she had to lie down again. She tried to remember what she must do to help herself. She was alone. There was no one within miles. She had no means of communication. The blessed feeling of having the day to herself had turned completely turtle. She braced herself for the ordeal. The spasms were widely spaced at first, but quickly became more frequent, and seemed to go on for ages. She could have screamed, and thought she must have done so on several occasions in the agony of the moment. She knew there was movement, but it was so barely perceptible, and so slow, and each time her whole system built up to a crescendo requiring her utmost strength. She was amazed at the strength she was able to muster, and after each spasm sank back on the bed in utter exhaustion, only to realise that she was on the brink of the next. Then suddenly, quite suddenly, it was all over, there was a rush of movement and all the pressure was off in one superhuman effort, and but for the pain of expulsion from her ravaged body, the relief was unimaginable. The baby was born. She gave herself over to a single moment's blessed relief, and as she did so, she suddenly realised that someone was watching her, male, an expression of bewilderment and alarm on his face. How long he had been there, she didn't know, but the door was wide open. It was Angus. It was unbelievable. But still she could not think of herself. She tried to lift herself from the pillow, and fell back, tried again: 'Please, Angus,' she pleaded.

Angus had heard Sue's cries the moment he set foot on the verandah. It was instinctive in him to try to be of assistance. A knock at Sue's door was drowned by a loud cry and a sob, and he opened the door and walked straight in. The baby was emerging. He had no idea what he must do or how he could help. Then she made her final effort and collapsed, and at last, she noticed him standing there. 'Please, Angus,' she whispered. He had no time for surprise, bewilderment, explanation. Sue's position was desperate, her need and tone urgent. He was of a practical, obedient nature, willing to help in every way he could, with whatever she wanted. She wanted the baby, and he straightaway lifted the child to her breast. It was damp and clammy, and as he raised it gingerly, it found air and commenced to bellow, and if he had been anybody but Angus the farmer's son, he might well have dropped it. It was a little girl such as he had never even imagined. There was much that was new to him that afterwards he could only wonder at the strangeness of it all, and wonder whether it was a dream or only his imagination, and the seeds of it lay in his mind to be pondered at his leisure.

With his timely and invaluable help, Sue was made more comfortable and settled down with her daughter for rest in earnest. After an hour's sleep, she bathed, changed her clothes, and did what she could to look as normal as possible. Angus was unable to wait any longer after she waked, and said he must be getting back to the paddock, because the sheep would be starting to move; it was 4 p.m. and the heat of the day had passed its peak. In the past hour, they had commenced to graze again and drink their fill at the dam.

On return to the flock, he moved round by the lake, gently mustering them, taking his time, so that by six they were headed generally for the gate. They passed into a long timbered strip a couple of chains wide between the paddocks to the west. It was half a mile or so the sheep had traversed many times passing to and from the yards. The sun's heat was still fierce but modulated as it filtered through the tall eucalypts. The sheep poured up the strip in a large viscous stream, raising fine dust with thousands of cloven hooves, and carving a network of narrow paths in the earth. Angus padded behind in his bare feet, the dry dust puffing up between his toes at every step. It was an unhurried journey; it was a contented, peaceful scene; the brown dust rose and wafted gently northward in the ghost of an evening breeze, and a soft, monotonous bleating emanated continuously from two thousand patient throats. It stood in sharp contrast to the urgency and relief, climax and anti-climax, emotional stress and quiet satisfaction of all of which he had just borne witness to, an unsolicited participant. It seemed as though the events of the day had opened his eyes to many things he had never even considered. By sundown the sheep were all safely behind railings, and shut up with swing gates, and he commenced the walk back to the house.

He found Sue in the kitchen, putting the final touches to an evening meal. She looked refreshed, though a little pale. He felt he should help her; he felt tired himself, and a little embarrassed in her presence, but he did not have long to wait until his Mum and Dad appeared, the carbide lights on the little sulky showing dimly in the fading twilight, and the familiar clip of the pony's shoes drawing nearer, till it stopped at the gate to allow Evelyn to alight. He ran out to meet them.

'Mum! Dad!' he called, 'Sue's not been very well.'

'Hello, son,' said his father, 'How are you? Are the sheep all right?'

'Yes, fine, Dad,' he answered.

'What is it, Angus?' asked his mother. 'Where is Sue?'

'She's in the kitchen, the baby has come.'

'Oh, my goodness; is she all right?'

'Er, I think so. Come and see her.' And at the door they met Sue with the baby in her arms.

Evelyn gushed over the baby girl. Sue wasn't allowed to do a thing; she must have complete rest, so Evelyn said. 'However did Sue manage all by herself?' she fluttered.

'Angus helped me,' said Sue. Alec raised his eyebrows at that, and gradually the whole story unfolded itself. Whatever they thought, the McAllisters withheld private concerns, and expressed only wonder, and pleasure in the knowledge that all was well that had ended well. Both were satisfied with the results of their own expedition, and but for the adjustments which must now be made to accommodate a new baby girl, things must proceed as before.

'Mum,' said Angus, as his mother tucked him into his verandah bed that night.

'Yes, dear, you've had a busy day. What excitement! What do you want to tell me?'

'Mum. I've been thinking; and I don't think I want to be a doctor when I grow up.'

Eveyln almost choked on the giggle which erupted in her chest, but with admirable self control, she answered, 'Don't you dear? Well, we'll talk about it another day. Goodnight, now, dear,' and she made haste indoors.

A Step In Time

Gabriel Schugg, of Cranthorne and Schugg, Barristers and Solicitors, Rundle Street, Adelaide, adjusted his pince-nez, and peered across the broad expanse of his office desk at the mild, greyish little woman sitting opposite him. She was alert, but not a little confused by the mass of material which he had been discussing with her, anxious to do the right thing, say the right thing, hoping that the information which she had been imparting in answer to his questions was accurate; it was in fact as accurate as she had been able to remember. She looked to him for signs of his satisfaction with it.

'Well, it's been a pleasure to meet you, Mrs Claverley,' he was saying, 'and however much it may have been an inconvenience to you to come down all this way, I have to assure you that it will expedite a conclusion to your husband's estate. We do like to deal personally with our clients – and get to know them; and now, I dare say, you will be wanting to get home as soon as you can – things to attend to I expect?'

He was a large man, of sturdy build, possibly from sitting too many hours in his office over cases just such as hers; in fact, the practice was known for the extent of its probate and conveyancing business. He had made her feel at home. She cast her eyes now over the sedate Edwardian furniture, comfortable, leather upholstered chairs, polished mahogany and glassed-in bookshelves packed with leather bound volumes. It was another world to her.

'Thank you, Mr Schugg,' she replied. 'I should be grateful if the business could be finished as soon as possible. It's been a bit of a shock, really, and I want to visit my daughter, as it's years since I saw her, and I've missed her so.'

'Ah, yes, your daughter, Western Australia, isn't she? Dear me, yes. The young people are adventurous, now, aren't they? Well, I have written to her, and will probably write again. So, if you are over there, I can write to you just as easily. Do you wish to go there now?'

'Is it all right to go there now?' Jennifer's heart took a bound.

'It certainly is.'

'Then I'll go ahead and get my ticket.'

'Yes, just let me know where you are and when you are back home again in case I need to contact you.'

Jennifer was elated. The interview was over, and when Mr Schugg bade her good afternoon at the door of his office, she thanked him enthusiastically, and went out into the city with a lighter step and a heart full of promise.

This was late January, and Mr Claverley had died in late spring, well before harvest. Their man on the farm had taken the crop off, and that busy time was behind her. Jennifer's husband had been twenty years her senior, but they had always been close, and she felt the loss keenly. Somehow, now that the harvest was over, the farm was unbearable to her. There seemed to be no future. They had four children, three boys and a girl; all were married; the two younger men had each presented her with two grandchildren. Her eldest was so far without issue; however, her daughter, who lived so far away, had a nine year old son whom she had never seen. Evelyn Claverley had visited Mildura all those years ago to make a social call. She had met Alec McAllister, who had dreams of going farming in Western Australia. She had fallen in love with his youthful good looks and his air of solidarity, and his talk of starting a new life in another state had inspired her. They married and took ship to Albany, then Fremantle. The Central Wheat Belt was their destination. They took up land under Conditional Purchase, worked and prospered, planning to return one day on a visit to her parents. They became absorbed into the routine of farm life, putting their energies into production and improvements and reaping good returns, so that the years slipped by with astonishing ease, it seemed almost unnoticeably, perhaps just because they were happy together, doing something worth while. The only real link, apart from camel train, with Adelaide, was by sea until the rail was completed.

It was a shock when she received the news of her father's death. In the innocence of youth, she had laboured under some sort of delusion that the present happy state would endure forever, and refused to see the writing which was surely on the wall. She was motivated to rush home to her mother. Such an interruption to their busy ordered existence would have been an undertaking indeed, but she was relieved of this anxiety when Alec arrived home from a periodic visit to their nearest town with a letter bearing an Adelaide postmark. It was a brief note from her mother to the effect that she was making the trip herself. Jennifer had not expected such freedom until her husband's estate was well and truly finalised, probably in twelve months time. Now, suddenly, she was liberated, and her excitement knew no bounds. She informed her daughter of her intentions immediately. Then she made her way back to her little farm, made her preparations, left her instructions, and departed once more for Port Augusta; with her mind in a whirl, she bought her ticket for Kalgoorlie. The Trans-Continental express was to leave the following day, and accordingly she was obliged to stay overnight in the town. She enquired at the ticket office about a hotel, and the clerk-in-attendance suggested she ask a cab-driver. There was only one cab, a hansom, to meet the country train she had arrived on.

'Sure, Madam,' replied the driver to her enquiry, 'an' if ye'll take my advice, ye'll go to the Port. It's the best place in town, an' they'll look afther ye foine.'

Jennifer warmed to his manner, and his Irish brogue was somehow reassuring. She was new to the business of travelling about the country, particularly on her own. She mentioned that she had to wait until the next day for the train to take her out west, and she asked him if he could take her to the hotel.

'Oi will, indade; an' arl, an' call for ye tomorrer, if ye don't mind the suggestion now.'

Jennifer said she would be very much obliged. It was comforting to have her accommodation and transfers settled so conveniently. He drove her to the Port Hotel, assisted her with her baggage and her booking, and she confidently placed herself in his hands for transport back to the station the following afternoon. She had before her two days and two nights travel to reach Kalgoorlie. Then she must take the Western Australian State rail to her daughter's home town. Sure enough the cabby turned up in good time for her to catch the express, and she was good and ready and waiting for him. He handed up the last of her bags to her at the carriage window, as the great train stood at the station.

'You've been very helpful,' she said. 'I have to come back this way in a few weeks. Do you think I could have you to help me again, if I need someone?'

'By arl means, Madam. Oi'm here every day. If you can't see me, just ask at the window for Mike. Mike's the name. They arl know me here.'

'Mike! Oh, all right, Mike. I'll remember that,'

'Ye'll not be stayin' long then. But ye'll like it over in the west. Oi'm told the people there are very friendly. An' Perth is a beautiful city, smarl, mind ye, but beautiful. That's the capital, ye know, on the River Swan. Oi've a son lives there, but he's a shearer, an' spends most of his time a-travellin' about the country. Are y' goin t' Perth, by any chance? Oi'd give ye his address, but he keeps a-changin' it,'

'I don't expect to be spending any time in Perth,' was her reply. 'My daughter lives away out in the country.'

'Aye, well probably not worth writin' it down. An' there goes the whistle. The station master's got the staff t' hand over, and he's wavin' the green flag. Ye're off! Good day t' ye, Madam, an' thankee f'r y'r business.'

The brakes came off, the engine gave a long blast of the siren, and an enormous spurt of steam issued in a cloud from the undercarriage, as the train commenced the journey which was to continue for eleven hundred miles. Jennifer's heart was full. She felt that she was going to the end of the earth. She reacted as though she was being farewelled by a dear relation whom she regarded as her last link with her former life. She waved and waved until the cabman was no more than a speck on the platform. Then she sank back on the seat of her compartment and took stock of herself. She was sixty-three, the mother and grandmother of families, a matriarch; she did not feel equal to the role; she felt that she was embarking on the greatest adventure of her life. The train moved inexorably beneath her, bearing her further afield every minute, the wheels monotonously sounding over the rail gaps – click-clack, in rhythmic repetition – eventually becoming totally absorbed in the new routine into which she herself was plunged. New scenery flew past her, countless square miles virtually uninhabited, treeless. The very emptiness exacerbated her sense of distance, the crossing of a continent, punctuated by infrequent halts at lonely settlements, sidings barely deserving the name, scarcely showing any sign of life – mainly natives from the desert who came in to meet the train in the hope of gifts of tobacco, sugar and tea. 'Bac – bac,' she would hear them calling from the platformless level beneath her window, as the train stood at the stops. She wished she had some to give them. She had three or four plugs of 'medium dark' at home, for her husband had smoked an ancient briar. If only she had known how much these fellows would have appreciated them, and how much she would have enjoyed giving it to them. It was a homely smell, the smoking of that medium dark, rich, pungent, pervading: she repented now her sometime irritation with its tendency occasionally to infiltrate her kitchen whilst she cooked an evening meal, or mingle with the bedroom aromas of sunbleached linen, talc powder, cold cream and carbolic – suddenly, she was overwhelmed by a desire to be back at home on the farm, but then, she would still be alone; she wished he were here with her now.

Mr Claverley had been a successful breadwinner in a modest way, on a small farm in the western slopes of the Flinders Ranges, growing crops, mainly of barley, with which he had supplied country breweries. They had been fortunate in avoiding many of the uncertainties of farm life, in a pocket area of assured rainfall, out of the way of the menace of bushfires, even in the midst of summer when the hot winds from the inland blew, searing both native and cultivated vegetation. They had been sufficient unto themselves during their lives together, saved their money, paid their debt, and achieved a reputation for being good, fair minded and agreeable. Jennifer, in particular, cherished her image of strict Victorian respectability and a proper standard of conduct. The demise of her partner in no way lessened her attachment to these qualities, and although she was now left with assets, a home, a farm, money in the bank, she was strangely at a loss as to the manner in which she might now journey into the future. What was she living for? Her grandchildren, those of her younger sons, lived so far away that, though she loved them very much, she saw them infrequently. It was a matter of aggravation that her daughter, with whom she had always had the most rapport, should live so very far away.

Over at the McAllisters the news of Jennifer's imminent arrival was received with mixed feelings. This was February, and she was expected by the 7th. Evelyn was in a spin. She was for the moment speechless, rendered completely powerless with excitement. Her mother's letters had hitherto been quite despairing of making the trip until the laborious winding up of the estate was well and truly over. The news of her imminent arrival was so sudden. For ten years, she had waited for a moment such as this, waited to reintroduce to her mother the man to whom she had entrusted her life, her 'baby' boy, the home and the lifestyle they had planned together way out in the bush like her mother before her, and the prospect of being able to share with her, even for so short a time, this vision of the future, was almost more than she could fairly contemplate. But where was she going to accommodate her? The house was so small, excellent in every way, but it contained only four rooms, only two of which were bedrooms, one a kitchen, one a sitting room. The latter was comfortable and homely with a large fireplace for use in winter. The kitchen was large and commodious, serving as dining hall as well as galley. The main bedroom was large and nicely furnished, but fully occupied by herself and her husband, and the second bedroom had been the home for years for Sue Gilming, now more than ever so since Sue had introduced into their household a new little stranger in the form of golden haired baby daughter Alicia. The child had from its first gasp breathed new life into the McAllister household – a good baby, a lucky mother.

There was so much to do, rearranging, cleaning, the latter in particular because it was the season of dust storms, and one in particular had coincided with the onset of the news. In that moment when she, Jennifer, realised she was free, without another thought she was descending upon them as fast as the Trans-Continental Express could deliver her thither. Angus, her grandson, was just starting school again after the Christmas holidays. He was just as excited and thrilled at the prospect of meeting his maternal grandmother, and rued the fact that he would be at lessons for most of her stay. His father was beset with misgivings and doubts as to the outcome of any extended association with the mother of the woman he had married; would she approve of him? She and he both would need to accept the situation as it was, so it was a matter of simply 'wait and see'. There was always the possibility that instant personal aversion might arise – Alec hoped not; he determined to anticipate the best of relationships with his, to him, unknown mother-in-law. He had been married long enough to learn from Evelyn that he was still, in Jennifer's eyes, an unknown quantity who had snared her daughter and taken her a thousand miles away, creating a barrier virtually preventing their reunion since, at least until the advent of the interstate rail link. The plans, so long at the backs of their minds, for them to take Angus to see his grandparents in South Australia, had never quite crystallised. He had done his best, he thought.

The fast approaching climax to all their expectations was not lost on Sue Gilming. It was obvious to her that there would not be room under that roof to fit in another occupant, even on a temporary basis. She had no hopes or expectations from Alicia's father. Beyond his name and his occupation, she knew nothing and she had done nothing to find out. He was just Pat Clohessy, the roving shearer's roustabout. She started to plan for another future, to include her baby. She could not regret a night of abandonment which had resulted in the advent of such a treasure of her very own. She would try for work in a country town, perhaps even in the city, where she could have her daughter with her, live in perhaps, if she was lucky, or perhaps, better still, with rooms of her own, a job to which she could take Alicia with her, to have access to her while she worked! A long shot, indeed, but one never knew. She had some money saved. The door to her present life was closing. Another would open. She was young, she was game, she would try anything. She imagined it was time to vacate her quarters, and perhaps sever forever her relationship with her employers. It meant giving up all the domesticity, the established habits, the comfort and security, the familiarity she had taken so much for granted. It mean ending endearing relationships she had forged for herself and Alicia; it meant going out into a hostile world armed with nothing but youth, health, strength and personality, meeting deprivation head on, a world without love, impersonal, uncaring. There was no other way. Her imagination did not contemplate a situation with permission for her to continue to occupy her comfortable room whilst her employer's mother slept in makeshift quarters. Overnight, she assembled her thoughts and her few possessions, and in the morning confronted Evelyn to give in her notice.

But Evelyn was appalled.

'Why are you doing this, Susan?' she demanded. She only ever called her Susan when she was under some stress herself. 'We thought you were satisfied with us. Have you got somewhere to go?' Concern for herself was intermingled with the same for Sue, since her helper had come to the farm when she was still very young. Evelyn had developed a genuine affection and a protective attitude towards her, as of a daughter. Their range of activities was so confined, their lives so interwoven, that she knew Sue could not have anywhere to go.

'I have to go, Mrs Mac,' said Sue, 'you're having a visitor, and I must give up my room. I could not expect not to.'

'Susan, I could not think of letting you go on that account. I – we need you, and will need you even more while Mother's here. We have never wanted you to go, and when you were expecting Alicia, we were on tenterhooks – if you'll forgive us – lest her father should come to claim you. We're very glad he hasn't, though we realise that's still a possibility.'

'Not very likely now, I would think,' said Sue.

'Well anyway, we're making plans to put Mother up, and those plans certainly include you. Please, Sue, won't you stay, and see us through this at least?'

'Well, then there's the baby. Won't your mother take exception to me? I wouldn't like it if she did to Alicia.'

'She'll probably adore her as much as we all do. Now, she'll only be here a month, at the most six weeks. I won't tell her anything, unless she's inquisitive, and that I don't think she will be, and when she gets to know you both, you need have no fears, even if she asks herself a few questions.'

'Oh, Mrs Mac, I do hope you're right.'

'I'm sure I am,' pursued Evelyn. 'There will be some inconveniences mainly because we only have two rooms. I wish we had a bigger house. The best we can offer you, since it all has to be done in such a hurry, is a screen down the centre of your room. You will have to use the door to the verandah, and Mother must use the door to the kitchen. Do you think you could put up with an arrangement like that for six weeks?'

'Yes,' said Sue, in a very small voice, and she turned and went back into her little room, considerably relieved, though at the same time, somewhat bewildered.

What if Alicia should disturb their guest in the night? What if Mrs Claverley should be dissatisfied with the arrangements for her accommodation? What if there were some embarrassing contretemps? What if she snored, or otherwise disturbed Sue's sleep, or Alicia's? A hundred unanswered questions filled Sue's mind, as she pondered the situation in which she would find herself in the next few weeks; and only time held the answers. In the following few days, the whole household was in some kind of limbo, a flutter of expectation and activity, and only Evelyn could have some notion of how things would develop.

But Jennifer was unquestioning of the conditions she might encounter on her arrival. For some years she had been accustomed to substantial comfort in the home she and her husband had built for themselves; but she had not forgotten the pioneer days, when necessity was so often quoted as the mother of invention, and she was quite prepared for most eventualities. It was a lonely sojourn on the train, for she had a sleeping compartment to herself, punctuated, as the time was, by meals and periodic visits from the steward; and the monotony of the scenery gave her the opportunity to sort out her jumbled thoughts, and for wondering anticipation. When the attendant informed her that the train had crossed the border, she was unable to discern any sign of it and concluded that there was none. The tiny settlements drifted past her window as before. The endless expanse continued until she reached Parkeston. This, she discovered, was a 'suburb' of Kalgoorlie, and here she must leave the comfortable, commodious Trans-Australian carriage to board the smaller West Australian Government Railway, on which she would continue her journey into the State of her daughter's adoption.

A soft, warm easterly blew gently across the halting place known as Nandine, where Evelyn waited with suppressed excitement, as the locomotive's headlights appeared over a distant rise and commenced the long descent onto the flats. It was three o'clock on the morning of 7 February 1920, and Alec had driven to the railhead with Evelyn in the family sulky. Neither had been to bed; Alec had put his head down for an hour in the evening. Evelyn hadn't had a wink; it just so happened that after all this time, she had become aware that she was expecting another baby: she would be exhausted, she knew, but then, she reflected constantly, it wasn't every day she would be seeing her mother again after ten years' absence. Alec promptly replied that it wasn't every day she expected an addition to the family. The thrill of anticipation kept her alive, and she kept Alec awake with her own restless energy.

The train levelled out a mile back along the track, and the headlight flooded the plain ahead of it, as the sound of its approach became audible and the long shrill blast of the whistle drifted into the darkness. In minutes it was beside them, and they could make out the barely distinguishable little figure of Jennifer leaning from the rail on the rear platform of her carriage. She was flanked by the conductor who assisted with the luggage and let down the steps. Then in a profusion of hugs, greetings, hugs, introductions and more hugs, interspersed with plaintive little utterances of delight, both talking at once, mother and daughter re-established contact and confirmed recognition of each other. How either ever paused long enough to comprehend what the other had just said was a mystery to Alec. The emotive intricacies of the fairer sex might remain forever an enigma for him. Perhaps it was a character trait subconsciously recognised by Evelyn in his basic attraction for her. After performing the first expected obeisances demanded of him by sheer courtesy he busied himself with Jennifer's modest baggage, receiving it from the conductor, checking it with their guest, and proceeding to load it into the tray of the sulky. The train moved off, leaving the ladies standing in the darkness like two chattering magpies, and despite the lateness of the hour, he experienced apparent reluctance from them, as he attempted to persuade them to move from the desolate station precincts and mount the steps of their waiting conveyance, immersed as they were in their continuing conversation. There were no lights now, only the lantern which he carried with him on these occasions. He extinguished this, mounted the driver's position on the right of the seat, took the reins, and with a word to the pony drove from the station yard onto the road home.

It was a long trip. The first five miles passed quickly, but by then conversation was waning. Jennifer might well have wondered how the little mare knew her way so well. The night was black, and there was nothing that she could identify. Dawn eventually spread her cool fingers with cautious first light across the sleeping countryside, disclosing the first features of Evelyn's chosen habitat, the dusty road, the wide wheatfields, now all standing in stubble, flocks of silently grazing sheep, partly cleared areas, patches of timber and vegetation alien to Jennifer. She maintained a conscious interest in everything, even the wide flat, open, featureless spaces not vastly different from the treeless plain she had just crossed. Eventually they passed along a couple of miles of road lined with mallee and drew up at the gates of the farm. The sleeping homestead lay half a mile within. Evelyn had nodded off against her husband's shoulder, and he glanced across at his mother-in-law as he disengaged himself from this modest encumbrance, and moved it gently in her direction. In the growing light, she winked at him. It was their first moment of empathy. She was, he reflected, not without a sense of humour, even at Evelyn's expense. He alighted to open the gate, led the pony and sulky through, and shut it behind them. In a few minutes they were at the garden fence. Evelyn woke instinctively at last. Sue was up, expecting them, with a fire in the grate, a pot of tea, and breakfast for those who wanted it, and she helped with the baggage. After Alec returned from taking the pony to the stables, Jennifer, Sue and he sat to porridge and toast. It was nearly 5 a.m. Evelyn was certain that if she had breakfast, she would immediately fall fast asleep. Angus, anxious to find out what his grandmother was like, soon joined them, and the usual comparisons were drawn between him and his forbears until he took himself off after growing mildly self-conscious.

Jennifer was at pains to discover all the facets of her daughter's life, and delighted to have been able to see her again after so long a separation. Having a daughter was to her, as to so many mothers, tantamount to having a friend, with the added benefit of kinship. Like so many of her ilk, she had imagined that friend living just around the corner, in the next street, within reasonably communicable distance, so that they could plan outings, arrange meetings, have discussions on subjects of mutual interest; not so close as to live in each other's pockets, nor so far as to negate all sorts of social contact. As in so many cases in real life, it had never worked out like that. This was her chance to amend that situation. She had made up her mind that she would make up for all those years when she had been the only woman on the farm, obliged to rely for sympathy and understanding on the men in her life, her husband and sons. With all the shortcomings of her present situation, they were more than compensated for by her delight in being able to re-establish the association she had felt she was entitled to.

She found Alec to be quiet, tolerant, reliable in an emergency, she thought, not always ready with a solution, but amenable to reason, and able to consider and reconsider alternatives. There arose between them a kind of mutual respect and understanding; and she thought, perhaps with a kind of quiet, amused, envy, that she realised the attraction he had for her daughter. There was little friction between the couple. Jennifer was glad, in the final analysis, that Evelyn had found so satisfactory a niche.

Altogether, her visit to the McAllister farm could not be counted less than a success. She had no responsibilities, and that alone, after a lifetime of managing her own household and bringing up four children with all that that entails, was holiday enough. She accepted without demur the curious sleeping arrangements. In fact she realised there was no other possibility. The proximity at night of Sue and the baby did not alarm or discomfort her. She might have well been used to babies once, though that was a facet of her youth, and she thought it unlikely to recur, save in the incidence of grandchildren. These, it is said, can always be handed back to the parents. She anticipated that having a twelve month old baby girl so close during the hours of slumber as behind a curtain might well have its problems. She was pleasantly surprised. Sue was careful to ensure that Alicia did not fuss after Jennifer had retired, or for that matter at any time. It required strict observance of feeding and sleeping times. Sue had always tried to ensure that the child was as little inconvenience to the family as possible.

Sue was subservient and, as they say, she knew her place; but she was not without character, and if asked her mind, gave her opinion as she saw it. Sometimes her opinion was very useful. She was accepted as an equal within the household. Jennifer was curious at first about her status, and of course about Alicia. She was aware, of course, that Sue had been there for several years. Evelyn had never told her mother about Alicia. What, thought Jennifer, was the child's origin? And who and where was the father? There was something about Sue's demeanour that suggested that it was Sue's business and nobody else's. Evelyn appeared to emanate the same message. Day after day, in the limited household precincts, in close communal contact, the three woman moved and lived and worked in an atmosphere of mutual trust and affection. It was such that after a month, no one wanted Jennifer to leave, and she herself was by no means in a hurry to return to her lonely life on the farm over a thousand miles away. Evelyn suggested that she stay for another fortnight, at least.

'Oh, but my dear, I mustn't stay any longer; I shall outstay my welcome!'

'Oh, Mother, I never heard anything so ridiculous. Why, we've all loved having you here, even Alicia, and when you go we'll all be desolate.'

Alicia might well have concluded, in fact, that Jennifer had become a permanent fixture in her life. Jennifer had attended to the child as often and as enthusiastically as her mother. There was nothing to rush home for, and her token resistance to the suggestion to extend her stay collapsed in ruins.

Most recognised, however, that a further two weeks was the limit, though her departure was marked by general regret on all fronts. There was life, indeed, for Jennifer, after her visit to Western Australia, as her thoughts began to marshal themselves in the solitude of her return journey. She must look into the future; there was Mr Schugg to revisit for news of progress of the estate; she would see Mike the cab-man again. She hoped she would have the opportunity of telling him about her visit, and give her opinion of Western Australia now that she had personal experience. She looked forward to meeting him again, and chid the monotony of the long journey as she awaited the train's slow return into Port Augusta junction.

Jennifer imagined herself to have become quite a traveller, as the result of her visit to another State, particularly the unknown and mysterious West. Why, up to three years before her journey, the only means of entry there was by sea, for few would have made the crossing by camel train. Born, and having spent all her life, in South Australia, she could only have guessed what life was like elsewhere. The sense of loss, abandonment and desolation brought about by the demise of her partner had seemed to her like the end of the world as she knew it. That was changed now. She looked into a brighter future. There was life to come, she would meet people, see things, go places. Her loneliness was replaced by itchy feet, a thirst to learn things and enjoy herself. Hitherto, she had never felt desire for personal experience; her pleasures had consisted in the service she had offered to others – the reflected satisfaction of making others happy. She was conscious, now, of the opportunities she had of something for herself.

She spent two days in Port Augusta, but she did not go to Adelaide, or make any move to contact Mr Schugg. The little town was mildly enlivened by an event in which she was able to play a minor role, and instead of returning to her home full of cares, and with the promise of work and worry, her heart was light, and her outlook was optimistic. The man whom she had left in charge was bewildered at her high spirits. She described the whole matter in a letter to her daughter as soon as she reached home and Evelyn read the letter a fortnight later in the quiet of her little sitting room after the family dinner in the evening.

My dearest Daughter [the letter ran] and her dear husband,

You cannot think what a lovely time I've had in your home, so many miles away, for the last six weeks. It does not seem nearly so far away now I've been there and stayed with you. You must have been quite put out when you realised I was coming so soon. I hope it was not too inconvenient for you. I can assure you that I was not in the least uncomfortable, or inconvenienced at any time. Sue must have been at great pains to ensure that. She is indeed an asset, and a friend, and you must convey to her my thanks for all her efforts. Her little daughter is a delight, and one day I must hope to renew my acquaintance with them.

Of course I have told you in detail with what apprehension I made the journey, and how in fact, it was uneventful save for one or two people I have met. Now I must tell you my bit of news. You remember the cab-driver at Port Augusta I told you about, and how helpful he was? I landed back there on the 'Trans', but had a couple of days to wait before my train went back up to Quorn, and so I asked at the ticket office for 'Mike', as he had told me. The ticket clerk told me he had been there earlier in the day, but was off on some personal errand, and would be back soon. So I waited, and sure enough, in about ten minutes he turned up. He was ever so pleased to see me, and I him, and he took me to my hotel as before. He seemed rather busy, and asked how long I would be staying, and when I said a couple of days, he said, 'O, but that'll be foine, just foine, because Oi'll be tied up termorrer, ye see, yes indade, Oi have to be at a weddin'. But the day afther, Oi'll pick yez up in good time for that train, Ma'am, an' thank ye.'

I said I was very pleased, and ventured to ask if it was a friend of his getting married.

'Well yes, it is. It's me son, Ma'am. The one that Oi told ye about, that's bin a shearin' in West Australia. He's decided to tie the knot, an' has come over here to do 't. Lovely girl, too, he's got. A pearler! Rosie! Just think o' 't. That bhoy o' mine. He lost his mother nearly ten years ago, an' he's been arl Oi had. Now, this toime termorrer, it's Mr and Mrs Pat Clohessy they'll be, fer sure.'

I made appreciative noises, and said that I knew what it was like to lose a partner,

'Aye, Ma'am,' he said, 'Oi'll be feelin' 't; but perhaps ye'd like t' see the weddin' an' arl. Could ye come now? Come as my guest – unless ye've somethun' better to do. Oi'd much appreciate y' comp'ny, t' be sure.'

Well, the long and the short of it is, that I did go with him, though I really didn't have an outfit suitable for a wedding. He was very attentive, and obviously very grateful for the company, It was a lovely wedding; the bride really was beautiful, and the groom so handsome with fair curly hair, and a face always smiling. He, my escort, was so proud to introduce them. We danced, yes, we danced, and went outside in the cool of the evening together. Then he took me, after it was all over, in his hansom to my hotel. It was the first time I'd really got outside myself since Dad died last September; and the next day he called to take me to my train. He wants to see me again, and when I said I wanted to go to Adelaide again soon, he wanted to go with me. He's really awfully nice. I really don't know what to do about all this. My dear, I think his intentions are serious, and I don't want to grow old all by myself.

It's been lovely seeing you again, my dear. Thank you so much for your hospitality, and I shall look forward to clearing things up here now, and perhaps seeing you all again soon. Or perhaps you'd rather pay me a visit. Coming back to the farm again after all the excitement seems a bit flat for the moment, but it is still my home, and I count my blessings. At least it's somewhere for all my boys and girls to come to see me whenever they want to, and it would be lovely to have you all home again.

I shall have to see the lawyers in Adelaide again soon. Mike will be with me for a while then, so it won't be such a lonesome trek as the last time. It will be something to look forward to.

All my love and good wishes, and hopes to see you both soon again. Ever your loving,

Mother.

Evelyn gasped, then caught herself. She had quite forgotten that Sue and Alec were both in the room with her. Both were in some sense, waiting for some news of her mother, and both turned heads sharply at the expression in her voice. It was too late. She was appalled, again. How could she tell Alec that her mother was perhaps romantically, involved? How could she let Sue know that her mother was friendly with her child's grandfather, that the baby's father was married to someone else?

For once in her life at least, Evelyn was glad that they were all so far away.

Ever After

The birth of Alicia was unregistered. It is true that Sue, her mother, was aware of the requirement. Naturally, of course, also were Evelyn and Alec McAllister, who in any event had a nine year old son. Sue rarely, if ever, went to town, and after Alicia arrived, besides being hindered by the responsibility of caring for a small child, she felt a reluctance to leave the farm, and continually postponed the chore of attending the court house and disclosing particulars of her baby's parentage. The result was that few outside her immediate associates were aware that she had given birth or even been expecting. Evelyn counselled her on the legal requirements, and she listened quietly and respectfully to her mistress's advice, but chose not to act on it, at least for the time being. If the truth were known, it did not weigh very heavily with her, nor, in fact, with either of her employers. In October 1920 Evelyn bore her second child, a bonny baby boy, somewhat to her dismay, perhaps, because she had wanted a daughter herself, but the presence in the house of Sue and Alicia considerably mollified any feelings she might have had of isolation, had she been the only woman on the farm, and she considered herself fortunate in having Sue's little family. Evelyn's new baby was duly registered and christened Bruce, but Sue remained non-compliant. Alicia was by this time coming up for her second birthday.

This mild increase in numbers in the McAllister homestead put pressure on the farmer to increase the size of the house. Evelyn's mother Jennifer had, with pioneering spirit, when Alicia was twelve months old, cheerfully accepted hastily contrived and severely limited accommodation for a short time at a moment's notice, but it was obvious, and in view of ensuing events, that there was only one way to go. The addition of extra rooms with improved facilities could, at that point in the decade be undertaken without too much difficulty, because prospects were good; and the McAllister community grew and prospered.

Jennifer Claverley did not make any further visits to West Australia, largely because she was now busy with her own affairs. She always intended to return, but she had been there and done it, and the importance of repeating the trip now gave way to other considerations. In any event Evelyn had promised to return on a visit to her childhood home as soon as Bruce was born. This was ostensibly to show her mother the new baby, but it was also a fact finding mission to discover how far her mother's association with Mike Clohessy had progressed. From correspondence it seemed that it was an enduring friendship. There was much to be done. She wished to meet Mr Clohessy and check him out for herself. She felt an obligation to ascertain, as nearly as she could, the likelihood of her mother's future security and happiness. Then, what was to become of the farm? She didn't know if her mother had made a will, and was vaguely aware that, in any event, it would be cancelled by a marriage. Really Jennifer could do what she liked with the farm, however disturbing it might appear to her children that her husband might be solely entitled to their childhood home, unless she made a will expressing some other intention. Three of her children were comfortably settled in their own homes with their spouses and children, and Evelyn and her two younger brothers might well have found consideration of another property to be an unwanted responsibility. Her oldest son Colville was not so favoured by fortune.

Colville was of a serious turn of mind, reflective, introspective, shy. By the date of the birth of Evelyn's second child, he was forty years of age. He had generally been regarded in his youth at school as clever. He did not show brilliance or top his class, but regularly came up with unique interpretations and surprising results, such that he might have been expected to undertake an academic, literary or clerical career. He showed no taste, however, for any course which might have taken him away from home, nor did he have any aptitude for farming. He worked for his father for a year after an ordinary primary school education. Then he took a position as cashier in a drapery store in the local town. In his late twenties he met his wife to be.

Olive Devine was a tallish slender woman with an arresting appearance and a dominant persuasive personality. She was a teacher in the tiny Government local primary school. There was one other teacher who had been appointed head. Olive was mainly concerned with the lower grades, but her colleague recognized her talents and it suited him to let her have *de facto* control of the whole school, not a vast regime to be sure, but enough to give her the opportunity to show her capabilities. The differences between them were significant. She was passionately fond of children; she looked forward to the school week, and allowed her duties to intrude well into her leisure time. He was a married man with children of his own, and regarded school only as a means of earning sufficient to support his family and it was with a blend of amused tolerance and personal relief that he allowed her to have her head in school affairs.

Upon Colville's initial encounter with Miss Devine he could not but be affected by her appearance. She was not a beautiful woman, but her delicately fair complexion might well have aroused the envy of others of her sex, and her face was crowned by a mass of flaming red hair. Her hazel eyes were kindly and alert. She was three years his junior. In all his life, Colville's mousey retiring nature had failed to make much impression on the opposite sex, and it was to his consummate surprise and gratification when this rather flamboyant lady fixed him with her attentions. She wanted a husband but above all she wanted children of her own. By and large, she was used to getting what she wanted.

The couple were happy enough for a time. The marriage gave Olive opportunity to explore the real purpose of her life. She was singularly unsuccessful. She lacked the ability to carry a child through to birth; time and again she lost the baby, till her body was drained and her spirit broke within her. She was so certain she could do it and so utterly desolate when she failed. For six years they lived together thus while she became progressively more miserable and querulous. Her fair skin dried to a yellow parchment in the warm air of the interior and disappointment twisted her features. In 1914 Colville joined the Australian Imperial Forces and was drafted overseas with an Ordnance unit. He was away for most of the war. Olive returned to teaching, but she had lost the will to live and in the winter of '17 succumbed to an attack of influenza. In 1919, Colville returned home to his former state of bachelordom.

When his father died his mother continued to rely on the services of a man of all work who had been employed on the farm for some years. She was aware that Colville did not have the stomach for farming and knew where she would be better served. Colville preferred to find his own way of living. He experimented with writing, letters to the newspapers, items of general interest, stories. He lived on the farm but took no part in the conduct of it and supplemented his deferred pay with a meagre income from literary contributions.

Evelyn arrived in January 1921. The farming communities usually found it convenient to take vacation after Christmas and harvest were done with. School children were on holiday and the lull in farm activity spelt a period of comparative leisure. It had been a satisfactory season. Primary produce was in demand: there was competition for the farmers' grain. Wool was still bringing a good price, if you had the sheep and the fences to contain them. Farmers had money to spend, and small towns sprang up in the outback; local agencies became established to improve contact between country customers and their requirements. The Government encouraged settlement by making land available on conditional purchase, favouring returned service men. Private buyers, ready enough to gamble on the world markets, competed for primary produce. Population in the outback areas increased; Alec McAllister was able to enlarge his holding and felt secure in doing so. It meant extra work and another employee but the times seemed to justify it. There was expansion in a general sense in South Australia also, and Evelyn found her mother much occupied with business, and making decisions of which she would never have thought her capable. 'Needs must when the devil drives,' she would say, if Evelyn deigned to query an apparently enigmatic course of action. The times were such, indeed, as to allow margin for error. She still found time to visit Port Augusta, not as frequently as she would like, but to maintain contact with her taxi driver friend. Colville still lived on the farm with Jennifer and she was glad of his company. At least, there was one member of the family who was able to give her the satisfactory feeling of being part of it. He was her oldest, and got on well with his mother. Evelyn was pleased to renew her ties with him; it had been such a long time they had been apart, and she was grateful that her mother had the company of her son. His contribution to the management and work of the farm was minimal, but at least he was self supporting and she could not feel alone in the world. He had accompanied her on jaunts to Port Augusta and he had met the family where lay her personal interest. She would ask him again, though Evelyn would be with her in any event, when she called on her friend. It was likely they would be asked to stay at his house. Evelyn thought the time was ripe to raise the subject of Alicia.

'Do you remember meeting Sue at our house, Mother?' she asked.

'Indeed I do. Your little helper. Yes, I liked her. Is she all right? How is she? And her little daughter?'

'She's very well, and so is the baby. She has been a great help, and good company, and she asked to be remembered to you.'

'Well, she's not leaving you, is she?'

'No, certainly not. I don't know what I'd do without her.'

'I'm very pleased to hear it. I'd like to meet her again.'

'I've been rather intrigued that you never enquired about the baby's father.'

'Yes, well, of course, it occurred to me, but I liked Sue. She was very nice to me, and I told myself it was none of my business.'

'I've always taken that attitude myself, I am in a position to know, however.'

'Perhaps. Is it important?'

'I think it's as well that we should know. Things have altered a bit since the baby was born.'

'Really! You're making it sound very mysterious. Why, who is the father then? I take it that Sue is unmarried.'

'Yes, she is. When the shearers came in 1918, there was a very nice young man in the team as rouseabout. Sue fell for him immediately, and he appeared to reciprocate her feelings. The team was only on the farm three days and has not been back since. It was during their stay that she became pregnant.'

'There is no doubt about it, then?'

'She said nothing to anyone about it, but of course there could be no doubt in anyone's mind, and eventually Sue told me sufficient to confirm the fact. Alec and I were, of course, very concerned that she would be leaving us. The baby's father has made no attempt to contact her, nor she him, however, so all our fears have been unnecessary. I would not have known his whereabouts myself, because shearers roam around all over the country, but I don't think she wants me to get in touch with him anyway. We've always kept her position secure and she feels at home with us.'

'Well, either he doesn't know about the baby or he doesn't want to know. Perhaps he should be told, however. He has a responsibility. He may want to know.'

'I think it may be too late! I believe he has since been married.'

'Oh, so you know something about him then. Do you know his name?' Evelyn continued in a conversational tone.

'He's called Pat Clohessy,' she said.

In the quiet reigning over the isolated homestead the angry scolding of a wagtail broke the silence of the afternoon.

'Pat Clohessy!' Jennifer said at last. It was a moment or two before she grasped its significance. 'But that's Mike's son's name. Was he ...? Did he ...? Is he ...? Her words trailed away.

'Well, Mother, I presume it's the same man, I think you told me that his son was in a shearing team in W.A.'

'Yes, indeed he was. Oh! poor Sue; and the poor child. Now she'll never have a father; what a coincidence! Who would believe this could happen.'

'I thought it proper to tell you, Mother, before you took any steps that might involve you. I thought it was bound to come out some time or another.'

'Well, I was going down this week. I wanted you to meet Mike. I think you would like him.' She didn't say that she was quite prepared to hear Mr Clohessy senior declare himself some time during her visit. She contented herself by saying, 'Now I must think what I must do; but I'll go down tomorrow in any event.'

The news sent Jennifer's blueprints back to the drawing board. Her background was Victorian but she could not permit it to interfere with an innate generous hearted spirit, nor to prevent her from accepting the unavoidable issues. She had maintained her association with Mr Clohessy, who had respected her widowed state and exhibited no questionable haste in furthering his alliance with her. He was a widower himself and, now his son was married, was alone in the world, so that he gave every indication that he would welcome the opportunity of having her as a partner. It would surely be disappointing to him if she were to refuse him, as indeed it would to her to have to do so. They were amply suited to one another. She was sixty four, comfortably off, active and full of enthusiasm for life; he was eight years her senior, still self employed and likewise in good health. Should they discard this opportunity for their mutual future? If she married Mike, assuming that he would ask her (though in her woman's mind she had little doubt of it) she would be in some kind of relationship (clandestinely, perhaps) to Alicia (a kind of step-grandmother, she thought) and she relished the thought as an attractive prospect. Might it not give her the right to feel a moral responsibility towards the child? It would not do to mention anything of the sort to Mike. The idea of being able to do something for the little waif appealed to her maternal sense. Her relationship to the child's father was a matter for concern. What were the chances of his meeting Sue again? If he remained in his chosen occupation, she must try to ensure that he could never again obtain work at her son-in-law's farm. If he ever discovered the truth, could he ever make things difficult for her, his father's new wife, his mother-in-law? Jennifer was hopeful that would not happen. It was just, she reasoned, one of the risks one might encounter from living on the planet.

These thoughts and many others ran through Jennifer's mind as she lay in her bed that evening. It was her intention to travel to Port Augusta the next day and she was not anxious to be shaken from this resolve. The information she had gleaned from Evelyn had had a decidedly sobering effect on her plans, and the ensuing conversation was marked by a preoccupation and thoughtfulness in her manner, which Evelyn expected, having regard to her mother's former enthusiasm and lightness of attitude, and respected. They whiled away the rest of the afternoon talking of minor subjects, and prepared for repose in the evening as usual without reference further to the subject which was uppermost in their minds. Before Jennifer fell asleep she had determined to ascertain if Mike Clohessy would take the opportunity, when they were together, to declare himself. What should she say – obey her feelings and accept, or play for time? The issues were not as yet clear cut.

Evelyn was relieved to find that there was no change in her mother's plans; she had no fault to find with the existing arrangement, and set about preparing herself and the baby for the journey. She wanted to meet Mike Clohessy, also his son and daughter-in-law if they should be available, and she was ready for any consequence which might ensue. For her the sooner these matters were resolved the better, since she could not prolong her stay indefinitely. At the appointed time they boarded the country train, and when they arrived at their destination it was late afternoon. Mike was expecting them.

'So this is the darthter Oi've heerd sae mich about!' he enthused as he assisted them from their compartment. 'Indade an' a foine lady she is, an' arl. Very pleased t' meet ye, Mrs McAllister!'

Evelyn did not know what to expect, but she was grateful for his friendliness, and she said, 'Please call me Evelyn.'

'Certainly, I will, with pleasure, an' I'm Mike t'everyone here.'

But Mike's genial exterior marked an inner being full of ongoing concern. He had lived in Australia several decades. With only basic skills he had discovered and sampled several opportunities before settling into one of his choice. Therein he had worked consistently if not hard, and prospered. He married, but his wife died leaving him with a boy about to enter his teens. He had few interests beyond his home, his stables and his equipment. The rooms had an empty sound when he returned to them. He endeavoured to assume a cheerful aspect in the presence of his son; many times afterwards he reflected that his assumed gaiety must have seemed as hollow as the house itself. He was not able to share his grief with the boy. Though he recognised his responsibilities, and made an effort to be a caring father, he could not regard his loss as other than a private one; the boy had perforce to do likewise. As time went on, the realisation mounted in his mind that his son was all he had left in the world, his own flesh and blood, the sole reminder of happier days. It was too late; in some curious way they had lived different lives. Young Pat left school a sturdy handsome youth of fifteen. There was not enough work in his father's business to employ them both. At seventeen he answered a request in the *Advertiser* for a young man to join a shearing team centred in the Eastern Wheatbelt of Western Australia. He was fired by the romance of adventure, and there was little doubt that he would be suitable. Mike was beset by doubts about his future, but there was no way he could see himself standing in the way of it, and Pat went forth to seek his own destiny. In the course of time Rosie crossed his path and he decided he wanted to marry her. She was drifting without apparent aim, and after a short period of courtship, decided she should accept him. She was 21 and he 22. He wrote to his father.

Mike was completely out of his depth on receiving a letter from Pat declaring these intentions. He had never stood in the way of anything constructive that his son had wanted to do, but this seemed preposterous. He had never received much news from Pat during his long period of absence, and though he had posted his own short letters more frequently, he often wondered whether, having regard to Pat's constant movement about the State, they ever reached him. Now Pat's letter informed him that he intended to set up house in Port Augusta. That would mean that he could have indirect contact, and someone at least in the vicinity whom he might call his own. He decided to discount any misgivings he harboured about his son's youth and immaturity. Shortly afterwards he made the acquaintance of Jennifer Claverley, who gave her impromptu consent to participate by being his partner in the celebratory event, and his loneliness somewhat abated.

Mike might well have had misgivings about the marriage: Pat did not abandon his chosen vocation, and was absent and away from his home as much as ever. It was as difficult to contact him and his communications were as wayward. It was difficult to sustain a marriage under such conditions and Rosie became increasingly unhappy. Pat's financial contributions were scanty and infrequent. She found it impossible to keep the rented apartment. Eventually Mike told her she should let it go, move into his house and be housekeeper to him. She was happy to do so. At least her livelihood was then assured and the move benefited both parties; Mike's house had not experienced a woman's touch for a decade.

With the passage of time it became apparent that Pat had grown weary of the marriage. Their several correspondence with him finally remained unanswered altogether. It seemed that he had concluded that the best way to deal with an unsatisfactory predicament was to pretend that it no longer existed. Rosie decided to forget about him. She was ready to direct her affections elsewhere. That was the situation which Jennifer discovered when she, Evelyn and Colville arrived on their visit in April 1922.

Jennifer was so obviously intrigued by the presence of Rosie in the house that Mike sensed her problem. After dinner the following evening he proposed they should take a drive out in a hansom. The three younger ones were left to their own devices. Mike drove her to a bayside area at that time of day deserted and they were able to converse unrestricted. He told her of the situation he was in and the events leading up to it.

'He's lost his mither, ye see, all these years, and not had the guidance she might have given. I haven't had the time to spend with him. I didn't know what was expected of me and now it's too late.'

'Mike,' she said, 'we know each other well enough now. You won't mind, I hope, if I say that I feel as though I were involved with you in their troubles, and I would like to help wherever I can.'

Jennifer's voice was gentle and coaxing. It was a tone she might have used to one of her sons if he had come to her with his troubles. He looked at her as if a weight had been lifted from his mind. At last, it seemed as if someone had come to share responsibility for this predicament, someone who understood and was ready to meet it head on.

'Jennifer,' he said, 'but ye're a comfort to me. Oi'll never forget yere willingness to come with me when I arst ye t' the weddin'. Jennifer,' he went on, as if he had suddenly gathered impetus from somewhere, from the company, from the drive, the outlook, the unburdening of his mind, all the poetry of the situation reacting on his Irish sentimentality. 'Oi wonder, now, could ye go with me? Oi've been meanin' t' ask ye for so long, an' never quite found the right occasion. Jennifer, could ye marry me?'

He was sitting half facing her across the front seat of the cab, reins in hand, head bowed as if ready for the worst, but still hoping for a favourable reply. She could have found it difficult to refuse him even if she'd wanted to.

'Mike,' she said, 'I think we should get along very well. Somehow I thought we would suit each other. Of course I had to wait to hear from you before I could determine what should happen to my own affairs. Besides, it would seem that you already have a very competent housekeeper. Do you think Rosie would want to stay with me in your house?'

'Rosie's a problem,' he replied. 'I could not see her struggling; she's become a member of the family, you know, and certainly, she's been a great help to me over the past weeks. But of course she must know that it can't be a permanent arrangement. Her place is with her husband, after all. I suppose we must bide our time to see what will become of this.'

He spoke with a spirit of resignation, as though his first burst of enthusiasm had met a set-back.

She met it with reassurance. 'We will wait together,' she comforted him.

But they did not have long to wait. Jennifer said nothing on their return to the house about the proposal which had been made to her, and Colville and Evelyn made no reference to her temporary absence. Three days later they returned to the farm; one week after their departure Pat arrived on one of his rare unscheduled random visits. This time he came with a purpose.

He had visited the apartment, where he had expected to see Rosie, but found it empty, with a TO LET sign in the window, and came thereafter to his father's house. It was 3.00 p.m. and Mike was at the railhead. Rosie answered the door, and gasped when she saw who the caller was, but there was no sign of pleasure or relief in either at the sight of the other. Rosie could only have been angry had he attempted conciliation. He laid his cards squarely on the table.

He was sorry that he had made such trouble for her, he said, he knew she must have had to give up the apartment; he had come as soon as he could to discover her circumstances, and was glad to find that his father had moved in to help. He did not want to resume marital relations, and asked her not to expect anything of him, because he had become involved with another woman and now she expected their baby. In a tide of humiliation, he confessed that he was entirely to blame for getting himself into this impossible position; there was no way out for him now but to remain with his new found partner and support her and her child.

Rosie met his expression of regret with ill concealed disbelief and listened to the tale of betrayal with obvious contempt. The fact that nothing more was expected from her was none the less a vast relief. The fact of the marriage was something with which she must deal at some future time. She did not want him to come into the house. She told him that his father was at the railway station if he wished to see him, and Pat left with the feeling that his connections with the past were irrevocably broken. When Mike returned later in the day Rosie appraised him of the morning's proceedings but Mike had not received a visit from his son.

'I wonder if I'll ever see him again now,' he said. Two weeks later he wrote a letter to Jennifer, relaying the incidents which had taken place.

'I'll not put her out,' he said, 'she's done nothing wrong, and nothing to upset me. Thinking it over, I wondered if we might go ahead with our plans, and hope that a suitable occupation might be found for her after all.'

But Jennifer was as yet unable to reply. She had no-one to confide in but her daughter. Evelyn had guessed that Mike had renewed his suit, but was unable to offer a solution, perhaps because she might be seen as an interested party. For when all was said and done, Jennifer could not disguise the fact that the farm was the main obstacle to her acceptance of Mike's offer. The farm was and had been for forty years her home, her life, her support and, since the loss of her husband, the source of her personal identity. She was a landowner, a person of substance, and she enjoyed the independence which it gave her. Colville depended on her for accommodation. There was mutual dependance for companionship. Evelyn was another matter; she had her own home and family; a few days after their return from Port Augusta, she departed for West Australia, expressing a wish that she could be present if the marriage should eventuate. She had by no means formed an unfavourable opinion of Mr Clohessy, and if the couple should see fit, she said, to spend time after the wedding with the McAllisters, then she would be more than pleased to have them. Jennifer was happy to receive the invitation, with private reservations however, since she was not quite ready for Mike and his grand-daughter to meet, nor for Sue to discover that he had one.

Following Evelyn's departure, Colville was again alone with his mother. If he had not already guessed it, he soon became aware of Jennifer's problems. Next to her, he was the person most to be affected if she should leave the farm. Neither could remain silent on the issue for very long.

'Do you propose to leave the farm, Mother?' he asked after dinner one evening. He introduced the subject in as tactful a manner as he could contrive, but in essence, the question, coming from the person who, next to his mother, was obviously most to be affected, also went to the core of the matter as it affected her, such that she knew immediately she didn't intend to leave the farm.

'No,' she replied, after the merest hint of hesitation.

He paused, not knowing precisely whether to continue. He did not feel entirely justified prying into his mother's affairs, but a curiosity born of intimate personal interest gave him the impetus to continue. It was not entirely her problem.

'Will you marry?' he ventured.

There was a short silence, then again, 'No.'

He knew she meant what she said. He wasn't satisfied with her answer however. He sensed that she was putting other considerations ahead of her own. He was determined that she should not put his interest first.

'You've no need to worry about me, Mother, you know. I can look after myself. All your life you've pandered to our wants. Now, at least it's time we considered yours. You must do what you want to, and we can take care of ourselves.'

She looked at him, her oldest child. He had not had an easy time: a tragic marriage, four years of war service, and now, no home, no apparent future; she would have to abandon him if she went to live in Port Augusta. Then her mind dwelt on the farm and her own home. They were sitting on a verandah facing east, looking at the range, misty blue in the distance, partly ringing the property in a low half circle, the creek lined with mallee, the familiar clumps of gums which had grown old in her lifetime, the paddocks of dried grass; she knew that this must be her destiny.

'I shall write to Mike tomorrow and thank him for his offer, and his patience. I can't keep him guessing.'

Ten days later Colville was obliged to go to Adelaide to discuss a matter with the editor of a magazine to which he contributed. On the way back he alighted from his carriage at Port Augusta and came face to face with Mike on the rail station. Colville was not an invasive person but Mike was pleased to meet him again, if only because he provided a link with Jennifer. His customary urbanity was obviously marked by some personal concern and Colville learned that he had received a letter from his mother.

'Bad news, was it?' he asked and Mike was ready to unburden his misfortunes. Colville proved himself used to the incidence of disappointment and showed a sympathetic turn of mind. Mike told him that he had hoped to make his mother happy.

'I'm sure,' said Colville, 'there must be a simple way of settling this, are you going to stay in business down here in Port Augusta?'

Mike had no definite answer to the question. He had fully expected that he would do so as long as he were able to mount the steps of a hansom. He had had some half-formed notion that his son might take over when he was too old to run the business, but that seemed now a lost dream. He was fond of Rosie, he said, and anxious to make up for his son's defection, but a woman could not handle things, besides, the hansom business was under threat from the motor car, which had begun to appear on the streets. People were bound to prefer motorised taxis, and if he invested in one, it would present added difficulties.

'Perhaps she could employ a man to help her,' suggested Colville, 'that is, of course, if you ever decided to retire. Mike,' he said familiarly, 'I think my mother is very fond of you, and I think it desirable that you should marry. It's the farm, chiefly, that's standing in her way. If she can't come to you, perhaps you could go to her.'

The suggestion immediately sparked Mike's interest and his eyes lit up. 'Man,' he said, 'you've got the germ of an idea. If the mountain won't come to Mohammed, eh? Indade, yes. But of course, I couldn't leave Rosie to fend for herself, now.' He regarded Colville quizzically. 'Would ye be interested in giving her a hand, I wonder?'

Colville smiled. His suggestion had run away with him a bit, and Mike had allowed his imagination unexpected freedom. But he knew that Jennifer would be happy to see him with a secure future, within communicable distance, with perhaps, someone to keep house for him. He had experience from Ordnance days of horses and their equipment. He hoped that Rosie would remain, because he had always admired her and would look forward to being her employee. 'Are you offering me the job?' he queried, but he had the feeling that Mike would be glad to hand the reins over to him, whether or not Rosie decided to stay.

The encounter fuelled Mike's hopes and he determined to set about pursuing them without delay. A short self-examination convinced him that he must plan the steps carefully and he determined to approach Rosie first to ascertain her feelings. That evening after he had disposed of the day's engagements, fed the horses and dined, and she had fairly completed her household duties, he opened the subject as they sat at leisure in the little room she designated as a parlour.

He was more than pleased, he said, with the assistance she had been able to give him over the recent months since her arrival at his house. He was past retiring age, and it was high time he made a change; he wanted to give up the responsibilities of the cab service, and he believed that she, with the help of a suitable employee, could take it over. She would not be required to undertake any outside work, simply keep the accounts, give appropriate instructions and attend to the housekeeping. For all of this she would be paid a generous remuneration. The employee would be paid separately. He required nothing else from her, merely the knowledge that the business remained a going concern. In the case of any deterioration he reserved the right to resume control. He hoped the offer would be satisfactory.

Rosie was certainly a competent housekeeper. She had method and took pride in her work. She was temperamentally suited to it. She was adamant, however, that she would not keep accounts or undertake responsibility for the business. On the mention that Colville Claverly was interested as a potential employee, she relented visibly, but asserted that he ought also to relieve her of managerial duties. She was quite satisfied with housekeeping alone.

Mike's enthusiasm was well and truly awakened. The events of the past months, his son's wedding, the marriage deterioration, and the addition of Rosie to his household, his proposal to Jennifer and what he had taken to be virtual acceptance followed by outright rejection, all these had a very unsettling effect on an otherwise placid nature. For months an agreeable outcome had flitted in his path like a will-o-the-wisp, and it was obviously still out there in the shadows, if only he could grasp it. He could gauge now that Rosie would be amenable to a situation tailored to her choice, and he intended to try to create it. He believed Colville would look after the business: after all, there was little extra to do to receive the monies, pay the bills and keep a record, and he trusted him without question. He wrote to advise him of the alteration in arrangements and ask his approval.

Colville, on receipt of the letter, was pleased the matter was approaching solution, and discussed the proposal with his mother. Jennifer was highly bemused with the negotiations, which, revolving as they had been round her as the planets the sun, had nevertheless been conducted without her knowledge. She felt, on a sudden, a sense of power and importance born of the knowledge that she was still regarded as an object of value. She thought again of Sue Gimling and her little daughter, little pieces of driftwood on the seas of inconsequence, she deemed them, dependent upon the goodwill, the whim, and the circumstances of Alec and Evelyn McAllister, who by the grace of God and their own dedication enjoyed a relative security. She considered Alicia particularly: a child without birth record, shortly to be required to attend school and be ushered into a world where identity was essential. She should be free, thought Jennifer, to go without hindrance, handicap or stain, born as she was through no fault of her own, probably to marry, perhaps to one of Evelyn's boys (she would like to be alive to see that, she mused), and the idea fired her imagination. Mike wanted to marry her; she envisaged him as a figure on her farm, a man to turn to in need, a constant companion. Colville would not be far away; it was obvious he would have security, a home, and competent feminine care. Jennifer was satisfied. She prepared herself for the arrival of a further letter of proposal from Mike.

But it did not come.

Mike was rubbing his hands with glee as he contemplated the progress of his plans to date. He had managed things perfectly so far. Come to think of it, he would rather see his business carried on by Colville, who had experience of these things, was older, and probably more reliable. Rosie was in her natural element, and to cap it all, they were mutually trustworthy, and fond of each other's company. He set himself to pen a letter to Jennifer, apprising her of the developments, and once more to ask her if she would have him. But before he had the letter couched in appropriate terms, fairly written, he received a missile in the post addressed to him.

It was from Pat. He opened it with trembling fingers. He was too old, he thought, to be assailed by any further shock. Perhaps the boy had something pleasant to tell him after all. The letter was a catalogue of repentance, humility and chagrin for the tangled web he had woven about himself, apology for the disgrace he had brought upon his father and his wife, and speculation as to whether she would ever take him back. The 'lady' with whom he had become involved in West Australia he said, had miscarried the child she had conceived, and now informed him that he was not, in any event, the father, thereby denying what she had formerly, when it suited her, affirmed, and now wanted nothing more to do with him. The wretched boy was desperate to renew his family association and was returning at once to listen to his father's advice and follow it to the best of his ability. The letter had taken a fortnight to arrive in Mike's hands.

Mike was aghast. Whenever it was, he thought, that he stood on the threshold of his own happiness, some exterior force intervened to frustrate him. He knew not if Pat would resume his approach to Rosie; he could not imagine Rosie even listening to him; he felt confident that she had made up her mind and thought her attitude fully justified; but what did the boy have in mind? Obviously, by now, there was no certainty about any of his own plans. Pat might be expected to arrive at any time. There was little likelihood he would be able to stay in the house. Mike set about revising the information he had prepared in his letter to Jennifer.

> You will forgive me, I hope, [he wrote] for resuming correspondence with you after you have signified that my hopes for a closer communion have collapsed, for I venture to hope that our friendship will remain, and I thought you might like to hear further news of me. The fact is that I have made an arrangement to retire from business, and to hand it over to another person to run for me. With this in mind I have talked to your son Colville who was very interested, and we have arranged so that I can retire as soon as he comes in. Rosie will stay to live in and keep house, so that he is simply replacing me. Both were very pleased with the prospect and are looking forward to running the concern together. It is a great satisfaction to me to see two people so happy with the arrangements. However, in the pattern of my numerous disappointments of late years, something has cropped up which bids fair to throw all my plans into disarray. It is my son again. He is arriving back here anyday and I don't know to what end.

Here he recounted the circumstances which had brought Pat to his decision. He went on:

> There is really nothing I can do for him. I can't let him into my affairs now I have promised them elsewhere, and Rosie wants

nothing to do with him. How I can be expected to deal with such problems, what I have done to deserve such a son, I cannot guess: my retirement appeared to be such a foregone conclusion not less than being a reward for a lifetime of application.

Well, I don't want to burden you with my problems, it just helps to have someone to talk to about them, and you have always listened to my complaints, etc.

Yours Mike.

Jennifer read Mike's letter several times. She could not interpret it other than as a cry for help, and she wanted to respond to it in a positive way. Pat was obviously due to arrive any day, if indeed he was to arrive at all. His previous record had not been such as to fill one with confidence. However the information was enough to galvanize her into action. She realised something must be done immediately and conclusively. A letter was not enough – not incisive, and might be misunderstood. Some definite aim was to be achieved. She determined to go straight to the heart of the problem. She summoned Colville and told him he must accompany her to Port Augusta. It was a matter of grave importance. He recognized her urgency and complied without question. They arrived on Mike's doorstep in the late afternoon of the following day.

He was surprised and delighted at their arrival. He was like a child to whom his fairy godmother had appeared to grant his every wish. Pat had already arrived, though Mike had deemed it unwise for him to stay at the house. Rosie vehemently expressed her distaste for the merest contact with him. Jennifer counselled an immediate conference but first she wished to enlighten Mike with some information of which he had been hitherto unaware.

'Your son,' she told him, 'is the father of a three year old little girl,' and she proceeded to recount the circumstances and the means by which this information had come to her notice.

Mike could hardly bring himself to believe his ears.

'So, at the weddin', you knew nothing of this?' he said as the truth dawned on him.

'Nothing at all,' she replied. 'If I had, would I have been justified in making it known beforehand, or in forever holding my peace, as the ceremony decrees? Actually, I think I might have laid the whole problem on your shoulders.'

'We will never know,' said Mike. 'I think I'm very glad I didn't have to make the choice. Fate has done the work for us, for the marriage has turned out to be a disaster.'

'We must talk to your boy and see what he intends to do about it,' said Jennifer.

In the course of their conversation with Pat, it emerged that there had been no intimacy between the marriage partners. Mike was disbelieving, but Jennifer determined to consult with Rosie.

'I was unavailable,' declared Rosie, 'and he was with me so seldom and always for such a little time.'

Jennifer nodded. She thought she understood. 'And now it seems to be too late,' she said, 'to have any thoughts of being man and wife. He appears to have made it impossible for you.'

And Rosie could only say 'Yes,' with conviction.

'With your permission,' continued Jennifer, 'I know a lawyer who could, I think, solve your problems for you. Do you mind if I discuss it with him?'

It was some little time before Jennifer was able to tell Pat that he was father to a four year old baby girl. She had in the meantime discussions with Evelyn and Alec McAllister, who proposed that he should meet again with Sue, and if she would still have him, they might start a life together. Jennifer realised her dream and financed the erection of a tiny house on the farm for them. Alec now had five thousand acres and needed a permanent worker.

Colville and Rosie were happy with the result and Mike, who had been hand in glove with Jennifer in all the proceedings, was finally convinced that his luck had changed at last ...